GARZA TWINS ◈ BOOK TWO

A KINGDOM BENEATH THE WAVES

GARZA TWINS • BOOK TWO

A KINGDOM BENEATH THE WAVES

DAVID BOWLES

A Kingdom Beneath the Waves
All Rights Reserved
ISBN-13: 978-1-925148-93-0
Copyright ©2016 David Bowles/IFWG Publishing
V1.0

Printed in Palatino Linotype, Maya Culpa, Cuprum

Melbourne, Australia
IFWG Publishing, Inc.
www.ifwgpublishing.com

ACKNOWLEDGEMENTS

First and foremost, my sincerest thanks to the Pura Belpré committee of the Association for Library Service to Children (ALSC), a division of the American Library Association, and the National Association to Promote Library and Information Services to Latinos and the Spanish-speaking (REFORMA). Their selection of *The Smoking Mirror* as a Belpré Author Honor Book was a humbling honor that made the editing and publication of *A Kingdom Beneath the Wave* especially exciting.

Of course, the book's success is not just due to my efforts. I owe a huge debt of gratitude to many people who have supported the Garza Twins series, believed in my work, read early drafts, reviewed, and otherwise given publicity to this quirky fantasy tale of shape-shifting Latino twins from a small Texas town.

I should single out Gerry Huntman and Louise Zedda-Sampson of IFWG Publishing, who believed in the project when two years of unsuccessful pitches had me losing hope. My friends Xavier Garza, Guadalupe García McCall, René Saldaña, Jr., and Jason Henderson were especially awesome in giving me tips and boosting my confidence, as were other authors and illustrators like Malín Alegría, Viola Canales, Carolyn Flores, Lupe Ruiz-Flores, Jan Seale, Jeanette Larson, and many more.

Exposure is key to a work's success, and I would be remiss not to tip my hat to the people who reviewed or otherwise helped promote the book: Rudy Ch. Garcia and *La Bloga*, Sabrina Vourvoulias and *AL DÍA News*, Olivia Fowler and *GeekaChicas*, Ernest Hogan, Gabino Iglesias and Amy Cummins. A very special shout-out goes to the entire community of Texas authors/illustrators and to the guy who often wrangles us together: Pat Anderson, who put copies of this book in the hands of a bunch of people. The community of librarians in the Rio Grande Valley deserves a huge hug, especially María Elena Anzaldúa Ovalle and Priscilla Celina Suárez. I cannot forget, of course, all the teachers, librarians, administrators and other staff at Donna Independent School District, with a specific mention of Efrén Ceniceros, who along with his wife Dora has always given my writing the moral support I needed from my town (and the town of the Garza twins).

Above all, thanks to my wife Angélica and my children: Helene, Charlene and Angelo. Without you guys, I'm nothing. Thanks for putting up with my long hours locked up in my study with the computer, typing away like mad. I love you more than life itself.

A note to readers: I have once again taken elements from Aztec and Maya mythology and built a fantasy universe from them. While the gods and creatures you'll find in these pages spring mainly from Mesoamerican belief, I have taken substantial liberties with their roles and stories. It is my hope that you will become as fascinated by them as I am, going off excitedly to research and read as much as you can.

Water was sacred to Mesoamerican peoples, not only because it sustained life, but because they saw rivers and lakes and oceans as a porous border between human and divine.

Are you ready? Go on, then—dive deep into the sea with Carol and Johnny. They have wonders to show you.

To Anaís and Missael Domínguez, *los mejores sobrinos del mundo*

CHAPTER ONE

Pablo Limón was a recent immigrant, short and very dark-skinned. The perfect target for a loser like Cody Smith, who stood looming over the kid in the main hall of Veterans Middle School, just outside the library, on the last day of classes before the Christmas break.

"I'm sorry, what was that, you dirty *mojo*? Learn freaking English, punk. You're in the US now."

Johnny Garza shook his head and walked up, throwing his arm around Cody as if they were best friends. "Hey, guys, what's up! Pablo, my *cuate*. *¿Cómo te va en las clases?*"

Pablo looked up at the taller boys. A smile crossed his face. "*Bien*, Johnny. I do fine."

"*Órale, pues*. Why don't you head on to class, buddy? Don't want Mr. Torres getting on your case. Social studies is holy to him."

Pablo nodded, trembling with relief, then hurried toward the sixth-grade wing.

"What's your freaking problem, Johnny?" Cody asked, trying to pull away.

Johnny leaned in close to his rival. "You need to stop picking on the little ones, you jerk. Feel me? And the next time you throw around racist remarks…"

"What? You'll beat the crap out of me? Whatever. My dad's the *mayor*, you freak."

With a smile, Johnny reached up and snatched a strand of hair from Cody's head.

"Ow!" the other boy hissed, rubbing his skull. "The hell did you do that for?"

"I need a strand of your hair for the *curandera* I'm going to hire to jinx you, moron, if I ever hear you call someone a *mojo* or *wetback* again."

"Yeah, you and your crazy family, you all probably know a ton of witches and weirdoes like that. No wonder your mom got kidnapped by the cartels. Just stay away from me, dude."

Johnny watched Cody stamp off down the eighth-grade hall. Deep inside, beast-like ferocity squirmed, hungry to leap out and exact justice.

Juan Ángel "Johnny" Garza, like his mother and twin sister, was a *nagual*—a shapeshifter capable of transforming into a jaguar. Right now the jaguar within wanted to pounce on the stuck-up blond jerk, give him the scare of his lifetime. But Johnny calmed his *tonal*, his animal self.

I've got a better idea.

Johnny could use the savage magic available to him as a twin shapeshifter to assume the shape of any creature if he touched its DNA—even a human. Ducking into the boys' bathroom, he stepped inside a stall and concentrated on the strand of Cody's hair, coaxing his tonal into taking on the new form.

A flood of confused emotions staggered him—he could feel the popular boy's insecurity, his parents' lack of affection toward him, his unrequited crush on an unexpected mutual friend. The cadences of his speech, his sneering way of looking down at everyone; these things were instantly accessible. If he wanted, he could dig deeper. But that wasn't the point of this particular prank. He had no desire to get to know the mayor's son any better than this.

After winking at his disturbing new reflection in the mirror, Johnny sauntered out, heading toward the portables on the far side of the school, where he would very likely bump into Aniceto Sainz, better known as "Hot Cheetos." Sainz had taken over the position of chief bully vacated by Miguel "Mickey Mouse" Maldonado, who had finally been promoted to high school after five years at Veterans.

Sure enough, Sainz was smoking a cigarette in the shadow of an empty portable classroom, sheltered from the light December drizzle by the rotting eaves.

"Hey, loser," Johnny called in Cody's higher, more grating voice. "Nobody smokes any more. It's pretty ghetto."

Hot Cheetos snapped his head up, glaring at Johnny/Cody. "*Pinche gringo.* You want me to rip your face off or something?"

"I'm just saying, homie. Don't get all salty on me. Think about your health, Hot Cheetos."

Tossing his cigarette aside, Sainz balled his hands into fists. "*Güey, ahorita vas a ver que* your health ain't all that good, neither."

"Boys?"

Rounding the corner came Ms. De Los Ángeles, a special education teacher. She crossed her arms across her chest and shook her head. "Aniceto, you know I come have tacos out here with Mrs. Paz during first period. Every day. How many times do I have to bust you smoking before you learn your lesson?"

"*Chale*, miss. I ain't smoking." He stepped on the cigarette, which had put itself out in the damp weeds already.

"Sure you're not. Get on to class, sir. Now."

As the hood grumpily complied, the tough but kind teacher turned to Johnny/Cody. "Mr. Smith, your father may be the mayor, but that certainly doesn't give you carte blanche to skip class and get into fights with dangerous boys. What were you thinking?"

"I'm sorry, Ms. De Los Ángeles. It won't happen again."

She raised an eyebrow. "Impressive. Your Spanish pronunciation certainly has improved. Just last week you were struggling with my last name."

Oops!

"Yes, well, practice makes perfect, ma'am! Mrs. Paz is a great Spanish teacher, too. But, uh, I'm really late for class now, so I'll see you, okay?"

He turned tail and hurried back inside the building, only to bump into his sister Carol beside the gym.

"God, Cody, watch where you're going!"

Without a word, Johnny kept walking, hoping she wouldn't suspect anything.

"Hey, wait!"

Johnny turned his head slightly.

It's you, isn't it? Carol said in his mind.

Telepathy was one of the other advantages of being twin shapeshifters.

Busted. How did you know?

Cody buys designer polo shirts for his uniform, not the cheap Old Navy stuff you prefer.

4

She caught up to him and grabbed his arm, whispering hoarsely, "This is the stupidest thing you've ever done, Johnny. Shapeshifting at school? Into another human being? I don't remember any of our training mentioning that as a particularly good idea."

Johnny glanced about. Seeing no one, he let his own human self come forward a bit.

Ugh. You look like a computer-morphed composite of Johnny and Cody. Come all the way forward, please.

"Could be useful," Johnny said aloud in a voice that also blended his and his rival's. "Dude! Crazy."

Before they reached the back hall and its cameras, he had returned to his normal form. He quietly explained what had happened with Pablo and his plan for vengeance.

"Johnny, I know it seems brave to you—heroic—but we made a deal with Mom and Dad. We're not supposed to use our magic unless it's absolutely necessary. You could've just as easily reported Cody."

"Or punched his lights out."

"Yeah, that makes a lot of sense, moron. Anyway, shush: the door's open."

Mr. Zamora paused, his hand pointing at the smartboard. "So you found him, did you, Carolina?"

"He's been feeling sick. He was still in the bathroom."

People giggled or smirked throughout the classroom. Johnny clutched his stomach dramatically. "Yeah, I may have to run back all of a sudden, sir. When duty calls, duty calls."

He made his way to his desk amid the laughter and annoyed redirection of his teacher. Hot Cheetos had made it back before him, and the boy was meticulously carving a gang symbol into his desk.

"Hey, Aniceto," Johnny whispered.

The hood's hollowed eyes glanced up at him.

"I just bumped into Cody Smith. He told me to tell you to remember his advice. Whatever that means."

The older boy muttered a string of obscenities in Spanish, and Johnny smiled to himself.

Justice is a dish best served spicy, Cody old friend. Kind of like Hot Cheetos. Merry Christmas, dude.

hen the last bell rang, there wasn't much time to enjoy that special feeling of freedom that comes right at the beginning of the holidays. Johnny slowed his hurried pace for a moment as he passed the front office, smiling impishly at the sight of a hangdog Cody Smith, slumped in a chair beside Hot Cheetos. A security guard stood over them, gesturing toward the principal's office. Cody reached into his jacket for his cell phone, but the guard snatched it away.

Your privilege doesn't mean jack today, buddy. That'll teach you.

Carol was standing at the doors, gesturing at him. "Come on, Johnny. You can gloat later. Mom's already packed our bags. She's waiting for us."

As they stepped outside, Johnny rolled his eyes. Their mother was leaning against her friend Angie Rea's black Ford F450, checking the time on her smart phone.

Angie was an artist and usually hauled her massive upcycled sculptures around in the gas-guzzler up and down the state of

Texas. But today, the Garza family luggage, even with their mother's ridiculous number of suitcases, seemed pretty meager in the large bed of the truck.

Carol kissed her mom and Angie on the cheek as they clambered in; Johnny smiled and gave a quick wave.

"Wow, your son, Verónica!" Angie exclaimed as she pulled away from the school. "Super tall and just a little stuck-up, huh?"

"Yeah, he dwarfs Carol now, doesn't he? Crazy growth spurts."

Trying to head off the probably embarrassing direction of this conversation, Johnny leaned forward and pecked Angie on the cheek. "Sorry, Ms. Rea. The other dudes. You know how it is. Middle school life is tough without them seeing you give kisses to your mom's best friend."

"No, *pos*, I understand, Johnny. You kids excited about flying to Manzanillo? I hear the beaches are better than Acapulco."

Carol gave a nervous laugh. "Well, I mean, except for the volcano erupting..."

"...and the drug cartels shooting police helicopters out of the sky..." added Johnny.

"...and all the hurricane damage along the coast," Carol concluded, "I'm sure it'll be fine."

Verónica Quintero de Garza craned her neck around to glare at her children. "And since we all are very excited to see *Papá* and hear about the discoveries he's making, none of those things are going to keep us away, *¿verdad, amores?*"

Smile angelically, he muttered in Carol's mind. He put his arm around her shoulder, and leaned his head against hers, a look of innocence on his face. *In unison, now...*

"*Claro que no, mamá,*" they said together.

Their mother arched an eyebrow and laid a finger against her nose.

Other than their parents, no one else had any clue as to the twin's secret abilities, or how they had used them six months ago to rescue their mother from the clutches of the Aztec god Tezcatlipoca in the bowels of the Underworld. Against all odds, working together and drawing on their family's deep love, the twins had foiled the god's twisted plan.

After they had returned to the living world, Johnny had refused to keep this secret from the man he admired most and he had become a jaguar in front of his father. Dr. Oscar Garza had been both surprised and relieved to learn that his wife and children were shapeshifters.

Then he had revealed that he, too, had been hiding something from them. At the age of seventeen, Oscar had been admitted into the Charter Palms Mental Health Center due to a nervous breakdown. He had spent more than a year institutionalized.

"I snapped," he had told them, tears on his face, "because I had been seeing things all my life. Hallucinations, I thought. Very real ones. After your grandfather abandoned us, things got worse. Weird visions plagued me. Supernatural stuff. And I knew, or thought I knew, that madness ran in the family. I…Forgive me for never telling you, but your Uncle Fernando and I have another brother, the middle boy, Samuel. When he was little, my parents put him in an institution. I haven't seen him since. I'm guessing he's still there. Point is, I figured whatever he had was in me, too."

Verónica had hugged him tightly then, and the twins had clung to him as well. Johnny's heart had ached for the man, adrift without much family, believing himself crazy. He had understood in that moment just how lucky he was to have such loving parents and sister.

"When I got out, I had to be a skeptic, you see. I had to be very empirical in my dealings with the world. 'Everything has a rational explanation,' I reminded myself constantly. So when you disappeared, Vero, *pues*, how could I allow myself to imagine? It was easier to blame the cartels."

"*Ay, amor*," their mother had cried. "Forgive me. If only I had been honest with you. Maybe your torment wouldn't have been as bad."

He had shushed her with a kiss; in that instant, life for the Garza family was transformed.

Back in the Rio Grande Valley, Verónica had done all she could to train her children in their new abilities, even though their magic was well beyond her own. And Johnny's father had returned to his studies of pre-Columbian Mexico with a new perspective and dogged determination to learn what he could to protect his loved ones from sinister plans, even with the hope of discovering powerful ancient artifacts.

So, when an amateur archaeologist had discovered a strange network of stone-lined tubes under the ancient ruins of El Chanal in the Mexican state of Colima, Dr. Garza had jumped at the offer to be part of the scholarly research team investigating.

He had been there three weeks already. In his email to his family, he had described the excitement of discovering that the tubes apparently linked an underground pool at the heart of the ritual complex to nearby rivers and lagoons.

"I'll explain more when you're here," he had written. "And then we'll enjoy some sun and surf, heh."

First, of course, came the plane ride. Angie dropped them off at the McAllen Miller International Airport, where they boarded a plane for Houston and then—after a ridiculous layover that gave Johnny time to watch a bunch of kitschy old cartoons on his tablet—another for Guadalajara.

"Flip you for the window seat," he told Carol as they struggled down the aisle. Luckily for him he won, and soon he was staring out over the glittering wing at the patchwork land, broken only by the twisting ribbon of the river, which connected distant mountains to the sea like a massive version of the tubes at El Chanal.

CHAPTER TWO

The plane touched down in Guadalajara after 8:00 pm. Though their father urged them over the phone to stay there the night, he should have known better. Carol's mom was a determined and highly impatient woman used to getting her way. She dug her designer heels in.

"No, Oscar. I don't care how late it is. We haven't seen you for almost three weeks. I don't plan on waiting any longer than I have to, so I've rented a car and I'm driving down tonight. It's just three hours or so, anyway. That's right. Mm-hmm. Just make sure the other room is ready. And ours better not be a mess when I get there. *Sí, yo también te quiero, amor.* But I'm on my way, got it?"

Carol was still smiling at this exchange when she cried "Shotgun!" and slid into the passenger seat of the Nissan X-Trail.

"Take it," Johnny replied with a yawn. "I'd rather stretch out in the back, catch some zees."

"If you fit, you mean, giant boy." She tried to hide her jealousy with these sorts of jabs, but it did irritate her that her twin now had about ten centimeters on her.

Bet I could shift myself some shorter legs if I tried. You could probably stretch your bones, too, Short Round.

I'll have you know I'm the second-tallest girl in eighth grade...Oh, wait. That was a doofy reference to some old TV show or something, wasn't it?

"Mom, Carol doesn't know anything about Indiana Jones."

Starting the car with a wry grin, Verónica shook her head. "It's no fair if you're going to have telepathic conversations around me. I miss the jokes. *Pero, ya,* with the dad you've got, Carol? You should watch those films."

Once they were past the city limits, it was generally too dark to appreciate the countryside. But as Johnny slipped into a light sleep, Carol let her tonal edge slightly forward, just enough to benefit from the night vision of her wolf eyes.

Even the impressive countryside couldn't erase her exhaustion, and Carol soon found herself in the midst of a strange dream. Her father was standing inside of some stone chamber carved with what seemed ancient Mesoamerican pictographs. At the center of the room, a dark pool of water began to bubble and overflow. Soon her father's shoes were covered, and the level kept rising.

When it had reached his waist, Dr. Garza looked right at her, but his eyes were wrong. The hazel had gone all glittery green. It took her a second to understand.

They were Tezcatlipoca's eyes, staring out at her from her father's face. He smiled a twisted smile and spoke in that cool, sociopathic voice.

"Are you ready, child? It is now your turn. Let us see how far you can be bent, Carolina."

The word echoed, mockingly. *Carolina. Carolina. Carolina.*

"Carolina!"

Carol snapped awake. "What, what?"

"Look out the window, honey. It's the volcano—it's active again."

There in the north the silhouette of Volcán de Colima was backlit by an orange glow, and narrow streams of lava oozed down its southern face.

"Johnny, you've got to see this," she said, turning in her seat and shaking him awake.

"That's, uh, still pretty far from Manzanillo, though, right?" he asked as the volcano faded into the night behind them.

"Oh, don't be scared, love," their mother said reassuringly. "You'll be quite safe."

Carol gave him a motherly look. "Don't worry, wittle boy."

"Dude, I'm not *scared*, I just don't want my awesome vacation ruined by a natural disaster."

"Riiiiight. I see." She winked at him and then stopped teasing. "No, I get you. I'm looking forward to ten uninterrupted days of surf and sand. We totally deserve it."

The quarter moon was dropping into the Pacific Ocean when they arrived in Manzanillo at a lovely hotel that overlooked Santiago Bay. Their dad, groggy but happy to see them, hugged everyone tightly and then showed the twins to their room.

"I'll be gone in the morning, but let's meet for dinner down at El Arrecife. It's a great little restaurant on the beach about a half-kilometer down the strand from here. Say, five o'clock?"

With that, their parents kissed them goodnight and left them to their own devices.

Vacation had officially begun.

The next morning, after a light breakfast, Carol went down to the beach with her mother and brother. She fell immediately in love with the place, the curving sliver of beach overshadowed by thickly wooded cliffs and hills to which bright white buildings clung, precarious but stately. Johnny was predictably more excited by the engineering and architecture, but they both dove into the ocean as if born to it.

Can you imagine grabbing a shark's tooth or a bit of marlin bill and really exploring these bays? she thought at Johnny as they swam beneath the gentle waves.

Whoa, Carol! Watch out, there, you might actually have some fun with your magical powers.

Look, I know I get after you sometimes. But trust me—I want to explore our abilities more, too. I just don't want to involve any actual people in those experiments.

They spent most of the morning swimming and building (under Johnny's strict direction and their mother's keen eye) a vast castle of sand that towered like something from a fairytale, attracting many admiring glances from other tourists. But as they played, they continued to exchange ideas for how to get their parents to allow them to shift into aquatic animals at some point during the vacation.

Exhausted and hungry, they had lunch on the patio of the hotel's restaurant.

"Why don't you kids go shower and take a nap or something? I'm going shopping for a bit, but I'll meet you in the lobby at four-thirty." Giving each a quick peck on the cheek, their mother set off to engage in one of her favorite pastimes. Carol was tempted to join her, especially since she'd promised her friends cool mementos upon her return, but her muscles ached and she was crusted with sand and salt.

There'll be plenty of time for shopping, she thought to herself. *No reason to rush things.*

‌᠎᠎᠎᠎᠎᠎᠎᠎᠎᠎᠎᠎᠎᠎᠎᠎᠎

Carol woke up around 3:00 pm. Her brother was still fast asleep on the other bed, so she quietly pulled out her tablet and checked her email and social media. After updating Nikki, Sabrina and the rest about the gorgeous beach and waves, she posted a bunch of pics to her accounts, knowing how jealous everyone would be, given how cold it was in the Valley right now.

At 4:00 pm she woke Johnny and made him try to do something with his hair before they headed down to the lobby. Their mom was wearing an awesome new sundress and wide-brimmed hat, flipping through her smartphone apps as she waited for them. Together they walked along the beach, slipping sunglasses on to combat the glare of the setting sun on the Pacific's glassy blue-green swells. They found El Arrecife easily enough, and Carol selected a suitable *palapa;* the palm frond roof of the gazebo casting a perfect oval of shade across the outdoor table.

They had only just ordered their drinks when Dr. Garza came walking down from the parking lot and kissed them all on the crowns of their heads before dropping exhausted into his chair.

Before he had a chance to say much, the waiter plopped glasses and bottles down, and the family started to order, from ceviche to grilled barrel fish. It was going to be a banquet. Carol's mouth watered at the very thought.

"So," her dad began, "we spent most of the day with a bunch of high-tech equipment, mapping two new tunnels. You've seen the Mars rovers, right? Something like that. Don Cecilio was pretty dumbfounded."

"Don Cecilio?"

Dr. Garza looked over the rims of his glasses at his wife. "Oh, the local *viejito* who stumbled across the tunnels. Pretty useful for an amateur, even if he is a little nutty. Swears there are pink dolphins in the lagoons. Very strange. But look, what I want to show you are these."

He pulled out his tablet and opened the photo app. "Pass it around, Carol."

She looked at the bas-relief carvings her father had photographed, and something in her mind stirred. The figures were goggle-eyed and surrounded with water motifs. Very familiar. She handed the tablet to Johnny.

"So what are they?" she asked.

"Well, among the Nahua they were known as *tlaloqueh*, water elementals, sometimes given the title of *Ahuahqueh* or the Lords of Water. They were a bit like angels or demons, children and servants of the rain god Tlaloc, bringers of showers or storms, depending on his will. Our working theory is that this temple, with its central pool, was a place of sacrifice to the tlaloqueh to ensure crops had enough irrigation."

Johnny had given the tablet to their mom, and he now chimed in. "Okay, then. What role do the tunnels play? Why would they want to bring water from the lagoons? To, ugh, bleed victims into them from a distance?"

"Son, a year ago I would have probably theorized something

along those lines. But now I know, *we know*, that these elementals are probably real. So I'm thinking that the tunnels are *apiyaztli*—divine conduits that allowed minor gods to actually travel *into the temple itself* to receive the offerings."

"I am definitely going to use these as the basis for my next sculpture," their mother said, scrolling through the images. "They almost look like aliens."

"Don't they, though? And today's most exciting discovery is that one of the tubes stretches far beyond El Chanal, dozens of kilometers, in fact. We found a stone-and-mortar obstruction with human remains that seem to date back about 700 years. For some reason, the apiyaztli was deliberately blocked."

"Whoa," Johnny said appreciatively. "Must've been hard to keep the seawater held back long enough to build that."

"I'm betting they waited till low tide each day," Carol ventured. "What about the other tunnel? You said that you guys were working on two today."

"Ah, that one leads to Jabalí Lagoon, about thirteen minutes from the complex."

Carol heard her mother gasp softly. *"Laguna* Jabalí?"

"Yes, Vero. Why? Do you know something about it?"

"Well, when I was at the market near the town square, I asked around for stories of, uh, local monsters and so forth. A sort of heads-up, you see, in case there's something here we need to be prepared for. An elderly lady selling embroidery told me the tale of a creature living in that lagoon."

Their food was brought to them, heaping plates that Johnny assured everyone he could help empty with ease. Once the waiter had stepped away, Carol urged her mother to retell the legend.

"It might mean something, Mom. And you're so good at stories."

"Okay, you don't have to kiss up, silly. So here in Colima, near the town of Comala, the rivers that flow from the volcanoes and mountains have formed beautiful, mysterious lagoons like El Jabalí. From ancient times, apparently, weird tales have been passed down about supernatural things happening near these bodies of water—balls of fire, disembodied voices, flying witches. *Lo típico.* But the old woman assured me that strangest and most moving of these stories is that of the creature of Jabalí Lagoon.

"Years and years ago, while people were enjoying a beautiful spring day by the water's edge, a strong wind began to blow across the surface of the lake, sending unusual waves splashing against picnickers and bathers. The center of the lagoon began to bubble, and to everyone's surprise a strange creature emerged. It looked like a young man, but with the gills and fins of a fish, plus skin that glistened in the spring sunlight."

"Dude!" exclaimed Johnny with his mouth full of fish. "Like the *Creature from the Black Lagoon,* huh?"

Their mother laughed. "Pretty much, from what the woman said. It looked at the shocked humans with confused but equally astonished eyes. As it glanced all around, it was clear to the people of Comala that it meant them no harm. Maybe it had gotten lost. It didn't appear to have any idea where it was. Most people ran away in fear and swore they would never return. But some remained, trying to reassure the strange, scaly being. Over the next few weeks, many of them returned to visit. You see, it didn't leave. It had nowhere else to go, I guess. The oldest women, who still spoke the ancient tongues, claimed the creature was a, oh what did she call it? A tacami…tacamich…"

"*Tlacamichin*?" asked Dr. Garza.

"Yes! That's it. What does it mean?"

"It's Nahuatl for, uh, 'man-fish.' A mythological creature of some sort. Here, there were some grouped around one of the tlaloqueh in the temple…" He pulled up the picture, showed it to them again. "Looks like Johnny nailed it with his cinematic reference, huh?"

Carol recognized the creatures at once. "Johnny, aren't those the things we saw in Xibalba, skewering scorpions in that first river?"

"Oh, snap, you're right! I thought they looked familiar."

Carol turned back to her mother, eager to hear more. "And then, Mom?"

"Well, the elder women managed to communicate in a limited way with the stranger, and they learned of his deep sadness. He had lost his people centuries before, and in his endless searching he had forgotten his own name. When the children heard this, they began to call him Jabalí, after the name of the lagoon. A few parents who believed that Jabalí was good and meant no harm allowed their kids to splash around in the shallows close by. Their new friend taught them new ways to swim. As the weeks stretched into months, he became a deeply connected part of that community."

The fairytale rhythms of her mother's voice took Carol back to her childhood, when both she and Johnny would beg for a bedtime story every evening. It was strange to think that the longing she had once felt to be part of those legends, had been fulfilled not even a decade later in real life.

Still, something seemed to twist at the back of her mind, something she ought to remember. But her mother continued with the tale, and Carol ignored the nagging feeling.

"Finally the autumn wind rose, moaning across the water. Jabalí began to spend hours standing still under overhanging branches, listening. The wise women swore they could make out whispering, burbled voices in the wind speaking a language no human knew. Then one day, as suddenly as he had appeared, Jabalí was gone. The young ones, saddened, grew into men and women, and they told this tale to their children and their children's children. Now every spring boys and girls slip secretly to the lagoon to peer into its depths, hoping to see the creature. Many swear his face stares back up at them from the depths."

It was a sad and wondrous tale. Carol's eyes misted a bit as she imagined the lost being, searching down the long years for his people.

Johnny leaned forward. "Dad, maybe he found the apiyaztli. You guys should be careful, digging around in those tunnels. The man-fish might pop up and scare the crap out of one of your archeologist friends."

Everyone laughed at the mental image, then fell to eating and dissecting the legend in earnest, debating what connection there might have been before the Conquest among the tunnels, the tlacamichin, and the water elementals.

The sun was just a smear of red on the horizon when Dr. Garza paid the bill. The family took a walk along the beach, hand-in-hand under the stars and lovely quarter moon (though Carol had to explain several times to her argumentative brother that it wasn't called a half moon, technically, even though half its face was aglow).

They were resting contentedly among some boulders when the sand exploded upward just a few meters away. Their mother pushed her husband behind her, eyes shimmering with her tonal's eager energy. Carol and Johnny tensed up, ready to transform as well.

"Wait!" came a familiar voice. A small, child-like hand emerged from the new crater in the sand, and the most unexpected figure pulled itself out into the moonlight.

It was Pingo, one of the *tzapame*, the Little People. He brushed sand from his wild black hair and loincloth. He gave a slight bow.

"Howdy, Garza family! Sorry to barge into your holiday, but we've got us a little problem. And by 'us' I mean 'the entire planet,' folks."

CHAPTER THREE

Johnny sighed. "Well there goes our fun in the sun, every-body."

Dr. Garza looked at the being that had just crawled out of the sand. "Wait, you're a *tzapatzin*, aren't you?"

Taking her husband's arm, Johnny's mother nodded. "That's Pingo, Oscar. He was one of my teachers, briefly."

Pingo gave a small smile. "It's good to see you again, Verónica. Wouldn't you know? Your orneriness has been passed down to your children."

"Hey, wait a minute!" Johnny objected. "Only Carol's ornery, dude!"

His sister ignored him. "It's Tezcatlipoca again, isn't it?"

Johnny hissed involuntarily through his teeth at the name.

Pingo's shoulders slumped with chagrin, exhaustion, or both.

"Can we sit down a spell?" the elven man asked. "I've been travelling for quite a piece. Even the tzapame need their rest."

That's hundreds of kilometers, Johnny thought to himself. *Whatever drove him to find us here must be pretty bad.*

There was a part of him that grew more excited by the minute—the part that had been itching for a new challenge. And if the Lord of Chaos was behind the threat, so much the better.

I'd love another crack at the jerk.

All five of them sat cross-legged in a rough circle, partially shielded from prying eyes by a tumble of boulders. Pingo pulled a small stone from a pouch. After he mumbled a few cryptic words, it began to glow, illuminating their faces creepily.

"Now, to begin with, you need to know that out yonder," he pointed at the Pacific, "carved into grottoes in the roots of San Benedicto Island, leagues beneath the surface, there is a merfolk kingdom called Tapachco."

Johnny raised an eyebrow. "Wait. Merfolk?"

"Yes. You know, tritons and sirens. Similar to men or Little People, but with fish-like—"

"No, I get what they are, Pingo. Mermaids and, uh, mermaid-men or whatever. I'm just a little freaked they exist."

Wow, really? Mermaid-men? It's mermen, *Johnny. Or tritons, like he just said.* Carol's voice in his head carried with it hints of exasperation and suppressed amusement.

"Sure they exist. They have for tens of thousands of years. You see, merfolk are survivors of the Fourth Age of the world."

"Like the giants before them," Johnny's father muttered in awe.

Pingo tilted his head in surprise and nodded soberly. "Yup. Like the mighty giants themselves, Doc, those dwindling remnants of the very first sun. Merfolk were once a lot like humans, but the Feathered One transformed them so they could survive the Deluge that destroyed the Fourth Age. Those close to these shores later had truck with the Nahua tribes, like my own folk did, and we older species use Nahuatl as a sort of *lingua-franca* amongst ourselves now. In that tongue, the merfolk of Tapachco call themselves the *Atlacah*."

Since assuming the form of Huitzilopochtli in his last adventure, Johnny had found—to his father and sister's great chagrin—that he now understood classical Nahuatl like a native.

"The Water Dwellers."

"Yes. Well, the Atlacah of Tapachco are ruled by a king and queen whose greatest treasure is their beloved children: Princess Anamacani and Prince Maxaltic. But Maxaltic, for reasons unclear to us, has gone rogue, plumb crazy. During the approach of the recent hurricane, he fled the kingdom and gathered together a dark army of beings: *ahuitzomeh*—water hounds, a shape Johnny knows from his adventures in the Underworld—as well as *tlacamichimeh*—"

"We were just talking about them," Carol interrupted. "Scaly man-fish."

"I reckon that's a good description, sure. And *wayxocob*—deadly smart sharks. Rumor is that Maxaltic has recruited them to help him find the *Cehuallocozcatl*, the Shadow Stone, which was used thousands of years ago to sink the ancient nation of Atlan and nearly flood the world."

Carol visibly shuddered at the weapon's name. Johnny's gut clenched as he remembered the shadow magic that had almost overwhelmed her in Mictlan.

"Apparently," Pingo went on, "the prince believes he can use this jewel to unite merfolk and all other sentient marine beings against humanity. Celic—the hermit triton who shared this information with my elders—reckons he wants to flood the world again. We tzapame have reflected on what you two discovered in Mictlan, and our leaders figure that Maxaltic is being manipulated by water elementals under orders from Tezcatlipoca."

"I *knew* it," Carol whispered, averting her face for a moment. When she looked back at Pingo, there were tears in her eyes, but her jaw was set firmly. "How do we stop him?"

Johnny wanted to high-five her. *My sister freaking rocks.*

"You've got to go down there, you and Johnny. To Tapachco. You've got to convince the King and Queen to send an army against their son. You've got to fight alongside them, and use your powers to make sure Maxaltic never gets his hands on the Shadow Stone. Our elders have called on the Feathered One, and he has...let them know that you will once again be aided in the hour of your greatest need."

Mrs. Garza drew a sharp breath. "That doesn't make me feel very confident, Pingo, about sending my thirteen-year-old children into the depths of the sea."

"I understand, Verónica. I've brought a few items." From his leather sack, the *tzapatzin* drew out a necklace and bracelet, similar to what he'd given the twins that summer, strung with bone and teeth and other strange bits. "These should help you assume a shape for nearly any circumstance."

Johnny reached out and took his bracelet, slipping it over his right wrist.

I had forgotten how freaking awesome this feels, he thought to his sister, who was pulling her necklace over her unruly brown hair.

Amen to that.

Dr. Garza had been silent for a while. Looking at Johnny and Carol carefully, he shook his head. "It's not enough. What about protection? What about weapons?"

Pingo nodded. "I reckon there'll be weapons aplenty in Tapachco. But as for protection...If I know Johnny, he packed

Huitzilopochtli's cloak even for holiday."

"What? *M'ijo, ¿no te dije que dejaras esa cosa en casa?*"

Johnny prickled a little at this. "Yeah, Mom, like I'm going to leave a thousand-year-old magical cloak at the house back in Donna. I'm sure the home security system will keep it safe from demons and dark gods."

"Good," Pingo said, cutting off any further response. "I've brought something darn near the same for you, Carol—the Robe of Mayahuel."

He pulled a shimmering green garment from his bag and placed it in Carol's hands. It looked like layers and layers of sheer leaves woven together with ancient sorcery. Johnny had to admit it was beautiful.

"Oh, wow," Carol breathed as she lifted the robe, rubbing the fabric between her fingertips. "Look at how it catches the moon-light!"

"Mayahuel. She was the only *tzitzimitl* to reject destruction." Johnny was surprised at the reverence in his father's voice as he reached out to touch the robe. "She joined with Quetzalcoatl against her sisters."

Dr. Garza's hand clenched into a fist.

"But she was destroyed by those ancient star demons, Pingo. Can you swear to me that my daughter will be safer than she was?"

Pingo lifted his glowing stone as if to better see the man's face.

"I can swear no such thing, Oscar Garza. All our lives hang in the balance, partner, and who's to say what the future brings? But I will remind you of this—Mayahuel was destroyed, that she was.

But the Feathered One sealed her sisters up where they could do no more harm, then he gathered his beloved's bones and brought her back to life. Sure, sometimes we blessed creatures—children of his hands—teeter on the verge of despair at our weakness. But what can we do but our very best, trusting in those mightier than us to figure out the rest?"

"I just remembered something really important."

Johnny turned to look at Carol, whose face seemed unnaturally pale in the light of the moon and Pingo's magical rock.

"What, Sis?"

"I had a dream when we were driving here. It was you, Dad. You were inside the temple at El Chanal. The water started rising from the pool, getting higher and higher. Then it was like Tezcatlipoca was speaking through you."

Pingo turned sharply to face her. "What did he say?"

"Uh, something like, 'Are you ready, child? It's now your turn. Let's see how far you can bend.' I think...I think it has to do with the Shadow Stone. He knows how *cehualli* affects me. His shadow magic nearly killed me last time."

Their parents started shaking their heads and talking at once, telling Pingo to find other champions, forbidding the twins to go to Tapachco, generally freaking out. Carol was trying to reason with them. Their voices got louder and louder.

Johnny let them go on for a few seconds, shaking his head in disbelief. Then he had to yell. "That's *enough!* Shut up, all of you!"

Everyone fell silent and stared at him in shock.

"You're forgetting something. Tezcatlipoca isn't going to kill us. That's not his deal, hello. He wants to *use* us. He's trying to make us into weapons, remember? Talking about the star demons, he wants to bust them out. But he can't. Only savage magic can, and we're the only ones who've got it. So there aren't any other damn champions, Mom and Dad. And there won't be death, I'm betting. What there *will* be is a buttload of temptation and stress. But me and Carol? We got this. We *walked through nine levels of freaking hell together. We* are each other's defense, guys. Cloaks and swords and all are great, but I've got her back and she's got mine. So let's get this freaking show on the road before Prince Mazel-tov or whatever the hell his name is floods the world faster than global warming."

His dad glowered at him for a moment, and then his face relaxed. A tear ran down the side of his nose. "Oh, Juan Ángel, my son, you amazing man. Okay. You're right, of course."

Mrs. Garza took a little longer to unclench, but she finally nodded. "*Bien*. But your father and I aren't just going to sit on our hands. There has to be something we can do as well."

"There must be a reason Tezcatlipoca appeared to you in my form and at El Chanal, Carol. Waters rising…Maybe he wants to flood the tunnels for some purpose. To keep us from finding something? I'll dig into the lore, see whether there is a tool of some sort that can counteract the Shadow Stone. Maybe it's there, at the temple or in the apiyaztli."

"How do the twins get to San Benedict, Pingo? That's in the Revillagigedo Archipelago, isn't it? Almost a thousand kilometers off shore. Don't tell me you expect them to swim all that way!"

"No, Verónica, that would take entirely too long, and they would get lost right quick. They'll be going by boat. A group of Little People are making arrangements with a captain who lives nearby. His family had a long tradition of trading with the Atlacah, but in recent years they've been a mite cut-off from the merfolk. We're offering him a deal that'll turn their fortunes around. Lots of pearls in the sea, if you catch my meaning."

"That's still, what, a three-day journey? I'm going with them. Oscar? Did you hear me? That way we can do some last-minute training and practice, and I can make sure the boat stays there until they return to the surface."

Johnny knew his father wouldn't argue. There wouldn't have been any point, and besides, she was clearly right.

Instead, Dr. Garza stood and drew them all into an embrace.

"We never asked for this burden. But it's ours, Garza family. Together, we are stronger than we ever would be singly. Each in our own way, we're going to play a part in stopping this menace. Just remember how much we love one another, what we mean to one another. That'll sustain us, always."

By the second day at sea, Johnny had taught his sister how to use the robe and savage magic to clothe herself however she wanted. He had to admit she was better at this than he was, conjuring up clothes that would have looked pretty good hanging on racks in the swankiest of stores in La Plaza Mall.

Their mother put them through their paces a final time, having them quickly shift between forms and hold were-shapes in between till they were growling with exhaustion.

"Wow," she said, morphing into her human self behind a privacy screen where she had left her clothes, "this younger generation of naguales sure wimps out fast."

"Oh, no, you didn't," shot Johnny with a mischievous grin. "Smack-talking mom gives her kids a dressing down while getting dressed. Too bad you don't have any savage magic, huh, Mrs. Seasoned Jaguar?"

"I can't believe you went there," his mother said, laughing as she emerged. "Age jokes? That's scraping the bottom of the barrel, even for you, Juan Ángel. But, come on, you two. Shifting is hungry work."

As evening edged the sky darker, Johnny followed his mother and sister down from the sun deck of the *Estela de Mar*—the largish live-aboard boat that was carrying them to the Revillagigedo Islands—to the dining room on the lower deck. There they joined Captain Sandoval and his three sons—Rey, Arturo and Nelson—for dinner. The captain's brother, Cristóbal, had remained on the bridge.

"We should arrive in the early morning," Sandoval informed them in Spanish. "We have supplies for nearly a month at sea. Do you think that will be enough?"

Johnny swallowed his mouthful and nodded before his mother could respond. "Yes, sir. I'm sure we'll be done before that."

"But you said you have a secondary plan, correct?" his mother clarified. "Just in case?"

"Certainly. I have colleagues who would be willing to bring more fuel and food, should we need it."

"We won't," Johnny insisted.

The three young Sandoval men were silent, but like always, their eyes were wide as they shot furtive glances at Johnny and especially Carol.

Still weirded out by the shapeshifters. And I'm guessing they think Carol's cute or whatever. I'd tell them off, but she can handle herself fine without me butting in. Heck, they're probably already scared half-to-death of her after our practice sessions on the sun deck, heh.

"In any event," the captain continued, "once you have made contact with the merfolk, they can always send messengers to the surface to inform us of any delay. We can then make adjustments accordingly."

Carol nodded. "That makes sense. I've been meaning to ask, Captain—how did your family start this relationship with the Atlacah?"

"Well, you see, back before the Spanish Conquest, much of the state of Colima was part of the kingdom of Colliman, where lived the Tecos or Colimecas, my ancestors, who spoke a dialect of Nahuatl and were distantly related to the Aztecs. Now, the Colimecas had openly traded with the merfolk for centuries, but after Cortés came, that changed. King Colimotl struggled valiantly against the Spaniards, but in the end our nation fell. The king's eldest son, however, made a pact with the Atlacah to provide them with the dry-land goods they needed, an exclusive treaty that lasted for 500 years until some foolishness on the part of my father. Luckily for my family, this crisis affords us a chance to right that wrong and re-establish our agreement."

"Good," Johnny's mom said curtly. "You'll be motivated to stay until they're done with their mission."

"Yes, ma'am. Don't worry. We have no plans to abandon your children. That is not our way."

Johnny wasn't worried. If anyone could make the *Estela de Mar* stay in place till they returned, it was Verónica Quintero de Garza.

After a bit of stargazing—the night sky dazzled, undiminished by the glow of civilization—the three of them retired to their cabins.

Johnny knew he needed a good night's rest, but the prospect of heading into the unknown depths of the ocean kept him tossing and turning until the early morning hours. Not even the special playlist of aquatic-themed dubstep tunes he'd created could relax him enough.

His biggest concern was sleep. Not now, on the eve of the adventure, but once they were beneath the waves. In Mictlan, they avoided sleep. They had no need for it. But if they spent weeks underwater, they were going to have to.

And what if we shift into human form once we're dreaming? We'll drown, be crushed by the pressure.

Finally, he had an idea. He sought his tonal, finding his animal soul quiescent deep within him. He nudged it forward, gave it control, but told it to sleep. Then he drifted into the calm formlessness of his deepest self and knew nothing more for a time.

Johnny! Johnny, what the heck, man? Why are you shifted into a jaguar? Wake up! We're here. Time to get moving.

He pulled himself to the surface of his mind, twisted the cloak into loose-fitting pajamas and became a teenage boy again.

"Hey," he said aloud with a yawn. "I solved the sleeping problem, Carol. No risk of drowning when your tonal is in charge and goes to sleep."

"Oh. I hadn't thought of that," she said. "Smart. But come on, man. They're waiting for us up on deck. Showtime."

They clambered up ladders to the sun deck. Shrouded in mist to starboard was San Benedicto Island, a sandy brown mass of rocky cliffs teeming with birds. The sea around them glittered like liquid turquoise. Johnny felt a shiver of awe—a sense of destiny—dance along his nerves.

"Okay," his mother said, leaning in close to the twins. "This is it. I won't tell you to be safe, to stay out of danger, because the whole point of this is for you to face a danger the rest of us can't. But stay together and rely on each other like you've learned. You're smart, both of you, and you've got good hearts. Follow what you know is true. Pray to the Mother when you find yourself in need. May God bless and keep you, my beloved children. Now go. Go."

Johnny reached out and wiped a tear from her cheek. "Take care of yourself, Mom. We'll be back before you know it."

Carol gave her a hug and a kiss, and the twins descended a ladder into the warm Pacific. Treading water for a moment, Johnny raised an eyebrow at his sister.

"So, what do you think? Manta ray?"

She laughed. "Oh, you know it."

They each pinched a tooth between forefinger and thumb and shifted.

CHAPTER FOUR

Exhilarated, Carol dove deep, beating her broad pectoral fins like wings, water streaming through her gills. The ocean darkened, but her excellent eyes adjusted, and other senses kept her fully aware of her surroundings.

Beside her, Johnny also rocketed downward. He waggled his small dorsal fin as he pulled slightly ahead.

Pingo said there would be a vent about 500 meters down on the north side. See any sign of it yet, Sis?

No. I'm checking for bubbles. Water's getting colder, so you've got to figure the caverns are warmer and the outflow will stir up the ocean.

Yeah, okay. If you say so, Bill Nye.

She ignored his snark and continued to scan the widening roots of the island. After another five minutes she sensed rather than saw the opening, which was hidden beneath an outcropping.

We're here, Johnny. Follow me in.

They found themselves in a broad sort of slanting shaft, where they had to really beat their fins against the flow of the warm stream to advance. The descent seemed interminable, but just as Carol was beginning to wonder if this was the right entrance, they suddenly emerged into a vast semi-circular chamber, a kilometer long and twice that deep, which was brightly lit from below by magma streams. Strange coral reefs jutted regularly from the outer wall, broken here and there by glowing grottoes closer to the molten rock.

Dude. Her brother's mind flooded hers with excitement. *That's a city! They* grew *a city!*

Grew?

Yeah. That's living coral, shaped into buildings. And they were smart—they didn't put it on the inside wall.

I don't get how that's smart.

Well, it's probably part of the magma vent for the volcano. If they'd grown it there, any magma flowing up through it would fry their homes.

Ah, I see. Wow. Who's the science guy now, huh?

Well, I've been reading about this stuff in preparation, you know. I'm not a total *moron.*

That's good to know. She sent a wave of lighthearted laughter. *What do you say we swim closer, check things out?*

As they moved toward the city, Carol noticed a pair of grotesque, almost prehistoric creatures that resembled a cross between an eel and a dragon.

Oh, I saw a picture of these suckers, Johnny told her with undercurrents of apprehension. *Frilled sharks. Bad news.*

Something was wrong. The sharks appeared to shimmer into another shape for a moment. She looked more closely at them, focusing her *xoxal* as they twisted around to stare right back.

Johnny, those aren't sharks.

Suddenly weighted nets shot out from the predators, twisting around the twins. The illusion of the frilled sharks fell away, and Carol saw that they were really two fierce-looking mermen. They wore breastplates and armored gauntlets and were armed with javelins and other, stranger weapons. Their pale gray arms and faces were banded with the darker charcoal of their slick tails and backs. Coral green hair was close-cropped on their heads, revealing small, almost vestigial ears like a sea lion's. Wide, dark-blue eyes caught the gleam of the magma streams and shone like a cat's in the darkness.

Atlacah guards. She tried to remain calm as they approached. *Let's shift into ahuitzomeh.*

Ah, the five-handed water dog. Smart option.

Shifted, Carol used the almost simian fingers at the end of each leg and her tail to extricate herself from the netting. The guards, who had slowed upon witnessing the strange transformation, began to chitter, chirp, click and moan in some language that reminded Carol of both dolphin calls and whale song.

Johnny pointed at his tufted ears with the fingers of his left paw and then drew a finger across his neck. *Sorry, dudes. No speakee mermaidee.*

One of the guards drew back his javelin. Carol noticed its steel tip and understood one reason the Atlacah would trade with humans; there could be no metalworking here beneath the sea.

Raising her front legs in a human gesture of surrender, she urged Johnny to do the same. *We need to meet the Queen and King, anyway. Might as well turn ourselves in and have an escort, no?*

The second guard stopped his partner, and after a brief exchange, the pair drew close and indicated a direction with their spears. Carol nodded and began to swim, her brother beside her, both allowing themselves to be essentially herded toward the city.

As Tapachco loomed larger and larger, Carol was dumb-founded by how alien it was. Structures often lacked windows or doors, being instead dotted with irregular openings arranged in spiral patterns along their length. Closer inspection revealed that some "buildings" sported a kind of baleen-mesh on smaller openings that probably served to filter water the way screens did on human windows. Large, shell-like protrusions studded the more ornate coral complexes; those with delicate spires splayed in multiple directions like the quills of a porcupine.

One of these shells twisted aside at a series of clicks from a guard, revealing the entrance to the most majestic of the coral structures.

I'm betting this is the palace, Johnny thought at her.

Probably so. Let's hope they're taking us to the throne room or whatever. We don't have much time to waste trying to get an audience with the royal couple.

They swam through a vast antechamber in which guards and what seemed attendants moved about, performing inscrutable tasks in spherical alcoves that grew from the walls like fruit at the end of stems. The guards re-oriented themselves so that the outside of the grotto was "down." Carol, instinctively adjusting the buoyancy of her water-dog form, balanced herself between the tug of gravity and the upthrust of the water. Clearly the Atlacah had used all available angles and spatial orientations to build their city.

It's like being on a space station, Johnny remarked. *Since the buoyant force basically lets us cancel gravity underwater, construction and life in general can happen all over the place. Very cool.*

They were guided to a broad hall of bioluminescent coral that spiraled downward, narrowing as it went.

Like a neon nautilus, Carol. Bet it follows the golden ratio.

Is that weird architectural geometry talk?

Pretty much, yeah.

When the passage had become barely wide enough for two merfolk abreast, it opened onto an opulent space grown from the same glowing material and filled with perhaps a hundred beautiful atlacah. Dominating the chamber were two ornate half-spheres attached to the "ceiling" by jewel-encrusted stems. Within them floated restfully the sovereigns of Tapachco.

The Queen—Iztalli, Pingo had said she was called—was white with tenuous blue markings. Her luminescent blue dreadlocks were piled high upon her head, held in place by a coronet of gold in which pearls and diamonds had been set. Eyes of liquid azurite were widely set above her broad nose. Like the other sirens gathered in the throne room, she wore little beyond a shell-fringed girdle and a sort of shimmering yoke necklace that draped across her chest.

King Nextic had coral pink skin with darker, almost red rosettes that reminded Carol of a leopard's spots. His long hair, white shot through with pink, had been braided and bound with a sort of glittering wire, but his long goatee floated free. In addition to his heavy crown, he wore a ceremonial version of the armor the guards sported—a chest plate and belt from which hung weighted strips of tooled leather. Carol was reminded of a Roman general and his soldiers.

Around them, in smaller spheres grown from the floor or floating free, were sirens and tritons—clearly aristocrats from the richness of their ornamentation. Arranged along the vast, curving wall were a dozen guards, a mixture of female and male.

There was an immediate exchange of clicks, groans, chatter. The Queen turned her dark-blue eyes upon the twins, slowing her communication, but of course Carol couldn't understand.

We need to try something else, Johnny. She looked down at her necklace. The twins had done some Internet searching trying to figure out what forms were available. There were varied bits of matter from a half dozen aquatic species, including the yellowed phalanx bone of a dolphin. She didn't think that would be a very good option—a mammal at this depth, without air.

Before she could give much thought to making it work, Johnny shifted into a large shark to the astonishment of the gathered atlacah.

Uh, Sis, doesn't seem like these bad boys do much communicating.

He then transformed into a squid and began make his skin flicker between red and white in a complex pattern. Guards swam toward him, spears at the ready.

They don't seem to understand me, heh. Got any ideas, Carol?

Just a crazy one.

Focusing her savage magic like she would when singing, Carol expelled air from the *ahuitzotl's* multiple lungs, creating a tenuous bubble of pressurized air around herself. Then she shifted into dolphin form and whistled a quick message.

"Not enemies! Friends!"

But that was all she could manage before the pressure of the sea threatened to crush her. She became a sort of octopus to survive.

The King surged from his spherical throne, gesturing at the twins.

Good call, Carol. I think he understood you. But we can't be dolphins, not at these depths, huh?

No. Maybe eventually we'll figure out how to use xoxal to protect ourselves, but right now there's no way.

Okay. We have only one choice, then. Remember Cody? How I impersonated him? Grab the nearest mermaid, Sis. Time to cosplay Ariel like you've always wanted to.

He shot out a tentacle, seizing a guard and yanking a sucker full of hair. As other guards whistled warnings and moved toward him, Carol spun and found a particularly pretty siren with electric green hair and markings the shade of mint. Drawing her close despite the struggle, Carol more delicately pulled a single strand from her dreads and transformed, guiding Mayahuel's robe into the shape of beautiful, glittering yoke and girdle.

Immediately she was flooded with another life, another personality, thousands of conflicting memories and perceptions. Pushing the unfamiliar self down the way she would her tonal, Carol focused on her surroundings with the senses of her new form.

She realized she could hear the siren cursing her.

"How dare you take my form, you filthy witch! I demand you transform immediately back."

"Sorry!" Carol replied in the merfolk's tongue. She knew the name of the siren, both the native version and its Nahuatl equivalent, saw her long family history, knew of her betrothal to a triton she despised. "Forgive me, Lady Ellelli. Give me just a moment."

"How do you know my name? Oh, by the gods...do you know *everything*?"

"No," Carol lied. She wasn't planning on looking any deeper than she needed to. While Ellelli stared at her in horror, Carol brought enough of herself forward to alter her appearance, infusing the siren's features with her own, shortening the hair to match her accustomed unruly mop.

She spun to see Johnny doing essentially the same, his nose, eyes and chin displacing the face of a nearby guard with a shock of white hair and swirls of red upon coral on arms and tail.

"Can it be?" Queen Iztalli exclaimed. "Human shapeshifters, able to assume any form…Are you twins?"

"Yes, Your Majesty," Carol replied. "I'm…" She hesitated a moment. There was no way to pronounce her name in their language. But seconds ago, when she had said the name of the siren whose form she had stolen, she had mouthed the Nahuatl word "Ellelli" while whistle-clicking the merfolk equivalent. This strange convention came naturally; it was clearly the norm in Tapachco. She searched her new vocabulary for "free woman," which was pretty close to the meaning of *Carolina*. "I'm Carol."

Oh, I get it, Johnny muttered in her mind. *Juan means 'god-graced.'*

"And I'm Johnny," he added, mouthing his English name while making the right click and groan.

The King gave a low, chittering laugh. "Free and graced by the gods. Auspicious names. My guards tell me you perceive them fully despite their *tzaccayotl*."

He means their glamor, Carol shared. *Illusion.*

Yeah, I get it. They have a little magic. Disguises them. Keeps them from the prying eyes of our kind.

Carol moved her hand in a pattern that signaled agreement or affirmation. "Yes, Your Majesty. We have really only just begun to explore our savage magic. This must just be another of its benefits."

"Well, Carol," Iztalli interjected. "Our secrets are clearly open to you. We know something of twin shapeshifters, tales passed down the long millennia. You have assumed the shape of merfolk; you have access to our ways. You can see past our disguises. You can take on the form of sea creatures we would struggle to best. You will understand, then, our need to immediately know your purpose among us. Do you mean us harm? Should we seize you now and thrust you into the magma flows?"

"No!" Carol cried. "Definitely not. No thrusting into magma flows, please."

"Yeah," Johnny concurred. "We are totally *not* here to hurt anyone, so it'd be really cool if you didn't hurt us, okay?"

"If you are not here to cause mischief," said a new voice, "then speak of your purpose. For years now we have spurned the human world. Why would your people send you now?"

Carol turned to find an older siren with a scar crossing her dark green features and an ornate helm covering her head. The patterned traceries in her armor were different from those of the guards. A quick peek into Elleli's memories told Carol these signaled the siren's high rank.

"This is our castellan, Nalquiza," the King explained. "She commands the Royal Guard."

"Oh, you've misunderstood, Castellan," Carol said. "Humans don't know you exist."

Johnny laughed. "Well, some crazy folks think you might. That fake report on *Animal Planet* didn't help much."

Shut up. This is really not the time for jokes. And you can't just twist their language like that. They don't know what 'World of the Animals' is, weirdo.

Carol turned her eyes on the sovereigns of Tapachco. "The tzapame sent us."

The light buzz of conversation among the courtiers died immediately. The Queen blinked rapidly for a few seconds.

"We must have proof of this claim, Carol."

Johnny spoke up before she could respond. "That's easy enough. They're required to send aid, aren't they, when one of the other magic races is in grave danger? Those were the terms set down at the beginning of this age by the Feathered One himself in the *Nenotzalli In Tlayocoltzin,* the Compact of Blessed Creatures. That ancient treaty doesn't give the Little People much choice. And since there are darker forces than you can imagine behind your son's betrayal, well, they decided to send in the big guns. Us."

Arrogant much?

It's the freaking truth, Carol. Pingo himself said all this to us.

Still. Don't get too stuck up about it.

"Our son." The Queen looked at her husband for a moment. He stared back at her impassively. To Carol they both seemed devastated despite their haughty expressions. "Tell me, human twins, what is it you would have us do about Prince Maxaltic? He has abandoned Tapachco, fleeing his impending union with the princess of Qucha Llaqta and with it our chance at controlling the Eastern Pacific. Rumor has it he has instead taken up with dark beings beyond our border. Though it pains me more than words can express, he is beyond redemption."

Carol shuddered at the sadness of those words. "Queen Iztalli, first of all, I don't believe that people are ever really beyond saving. There's always a chance, no matter how small, that they can see how wrong they are and turn away from the path they're on. But forget that for a second. The problem with

Maxaltic is bigger than just Tapachco and the royal family. He didn't leave to avoid a marriage—he's after the Shadow Stone."

Groans of dismay and horror came from all around the throne room. Guards gripped their weapons tightly, cast their eyes about as if searching for enemies.

The King dove toward Carol, his eyes wide with fury and despair. "Why would my son covet that evil device? Why would he court destruction in such a way?"

"He wants to flood the world. To destroy humanity. To unite the races of the sea and set himself up as their absolute ruler."

Now the Queen emerged from her throne, as if being closer to the bearers of bad tidings made the news more credible. "Insanity. No member of the House of Napotza would willingly do such a thing."

"Well," Johnny said, "we're pretty sure he didn't come up with the idea himself. He's being manipulated by Tezcatlipoca."

Pandemonium erupted. Guards seized Carol, but she made no move to free herself. Creaking shouts came from aristocrats as the King gestured for calm with his stone scepter. Johnny shoved away lances, wove dense black armor from his cloak.

"Enough!"

It wasn't the Queen or King's bright voice that reverberated throughout the throne room, nor was it the castellan or any of her guards. Instead, a young siren swam into the midst of the confusion, the spitting image of the queen except for pale rosettes like those of the king. Even before noting the circlet on her brow, Carol knew this was Princess Anamacani.

Everyone became still, even the King and Queen.

"I know the idea is frightening," she said calmly, "but I

believe the twins. Before abandoning the kingdom, my brother sought me out to ask for a Retelling. He wanted to hear of the Fall of Atlan. As the Royal Historian, it was my duty to comply. When I spoke of the Shadow Stone, there was a bleak avidity in his eyes that I did not understand. Now we all do. Maxaltic has allied himself with chaos.

"So tell us, Carol and Johnny of Atlixco, the human realm— what can we hope to do against such a devastating force?"

Carol shuddered against her own will. "You need to raise an army and send it against the prince before he finds the Shadow Stone."

King Nextic's knuckles went white as he squeezed his scepter.

"What if we cannot stop him in time?"

Johnny's smile sent a chill of foreboding down Carol's spine. "Then you'll be glad that we tagged along. We've dealt with the plans of Mr. Smoking Mirror before. Stopped his little apocalypse down in the Underworld, in fact. If your army can just get us to Maxaltic and fight off his goons, we'll take care of the rest."

Something told Carol that, despite her brother's bravado, things weren't going to be that easy at all.

CHAPTER FIVE

Johnny hadn't been thrilled to be dismissed from the throne room while the King, Queen and their advisers consulted in private, and he had definitely objected to being separated from his sister so that their tours of the city would not be "complicated by any temptation to act without royal leave."

Still, Princess Anamacani was an intriguing, intelligent, and wryly amusing guide, so he kept his complaints to himself.

He also had to admit that she was pretty cute for a mermaid with blue dreads and spots. The thought made him vaguely uncomfortable, so he was sort of glad Carol was off with a different *atlacatl*. She would definitely tease him if she knew.

Anamacani led Johnny through the heart of the city, and his mind boggled at the incredible architecture they'd achieved without the constraints of normal up-down orientation or thousands of years of human construction practices. Twisting tunnels threaded like veins throughout the coral spires, providing private passage from building to building. Merfolk thronged together or swam from place to place with the same oblivious purpose you see people moving in human cities. Johnny tried to imagine the everyday routine of such beings. He figured there was school, work, play, church…

But I'm not here to learn about all the boring stuff they do. Bigger fish to fry. Heh. Gotta use that one on Carol.

"Would you like to see construction in progress?"

Johnny looked at the princess, giving a quick smile. "Sure! I'm curious about how you guys pull off these feats of engineering."

Surrounded by a half dozen aids and royal guards, they swam up and over a chunk of Tapachco, curving back into the city a little nearer to the magma streams. Teams of workers were tending coral gardens on the rocky outer wall.

"This is part of the Atempan district," Anamacani explained as they got closer. "Tapachco has experienced huge growth over the last sixty years since the eruption, especially out here on the edges of the city."

They slowed and drifted close to a team carefully binding coral to force it to grow in a vertical sheet. *The wall of some building,* Johnny guessed.

"Wow. How long does it take to grow a structure this way?"

Making a gesture of respect toward the princess, a strange salute that began with both palms against the forehead, a coral cultivator responded, "You must be one of the humans. The whole city trembles with news of your arrival. What you see before you is no ordinary bed of coral, sir. We have had thousands of years to breed *notapachicah*; properly fed and exposed to calcium-rich currents, it can grow a hand-span or more a week."

"Amazing," Johnny replied, his eyes running over the bindings and stakes, the bladders being used by workers to pump nutrients into the water flowing among the pale fields of coral. Unexpectedly, he found himself reaching out toward the nearest

cultivation, not with his hands, but with xoxal, the savage magic that was his birthright. The *teotl* inside the coral, its life force, responded to his questing touch. With a thrill of excitement, Johnny saw the connections inside the teeming colony, its will to grow, to tower, to seek the warmth and tenuous light of the magma streams.

Not fully understanding what he was doing, Johnny poured his will into the coral, coaxing it to defy nature, to exceed breeding.

The gaps in the short walls closed. They visibly began to grow before everyone's eyes. Ten centimeters. Twenty.

Creaking shouts of alarm came from all around, and Johnny pulled his power back. Engineers and workers rushed to examine the coral. Guards clenched their weapons tightly.

The princess was staring at him. "Was that you? How are you able to do such a thing?"

"Yeah, it was me, but I have no clue. Me and Carol, we've got this added set of abilities since we're twin naguales. Xoxal, they call it. Savage magic."

Her expression grew serious. "Ah. Yes, I know of this power. No one has wielded it for a thousand years or more. I doubt my parents truly appreciate the importance of your presence in Tapachco. You and your sister should receive a greater degree of respect."

Yeah, that's what I keep saying, he quipped to himself. But he refrained from being snarky. She was clearly on his side.

"Thanks. They're adults, though. That's what they do, right? Ignore teenagers because we haven't lived long enough to find wisdom or whatever."

Still pensive, she nodded in a general gesture of agreement. "Come. Let me show you the caves. Growing coral is important, but the truly vital crops are closer to the magma flows."

They dove past the city, her retinue in tow. The glowing bands loomed larger ahead of them, and the currents became stronger and warmer. One kilometer below Tapachco, they came upon a network of caverns. Guards at the entrance of each carefully checked caravans of sixgill sharks used to pull large nets full of harvested plants toward the city.

"Captain Xicol," Anamacani called as they floated closer. "Please accompany my handmaiden Ilancueh back to Tapachco. I need you two to find my cousin Mihuah and Carolina—kindly escort them here to meet us in the Cave of History."

One of her guards gave a salute in reply and gestured at the youngest of the aids. Together, they darted back the way the company had come.

The princess led the rest of them into the cavern complex. Johnny's jaw dropped at the extensive fields of kelp, seagrass, and other subaquatic plants. Growers and harvesters skimmed along the tops of the rows, glancing up briefly at the visitors passing overhead before returning to work.

"How many people live in Tapachco?" Johnny asked.

"Close to 12,000. We have crops growing in some ten caverns, with another dozen dedicated to fisheries and the care of other marine livestock. But there is a different reason I have brought you here. It is important you know what is at stake, given the information you brought us about my brother and his quest. If you are to truly aid us, you need the right context."

Intrigued, he followed closely as they swam for another

fifteen minutes, entering a vast chamber that was empty except for a group of guards. As Anamacani gave them instructions, Johnny looked up at the glowing circle of light above—it seemed as if the surface of the ocean were right overhead, and beyond he swore he could make out the blurry forms of shelves and furniture of the sort humans use.

"Come," the princess said, touching his arm. "You and I will enter the Cave of History alone."

Rocketing upwards after her, Johnny burst through the surface and into the stale, thin, cool air of a somewhat human-friendly grotto. Anamacani had hauled herself onto the rocks that formed a lip around the pool...

...and to Johnny's astonishment, she shapeshifted into a young human woman with dark skin and dreads, looking something like a cross between a Maori and an Aboriginal Australian.

She is still beautiful, he thought to himself.

"You...but...how?"

The princess smiled as she smoothed her garments over her new form and spoke to him in oddly accented Spanish. "I should have warned you, but I could not resist giving you a surprise. I am the royal family's *Ehcamatini* or Air Sage. Every generation one or two of us are born with the latent ability to assume human shape. Inevitably, the Air Sage becomes the Royal Historian, charged with keeping our people's chronicles safe and current. My Aunt Omelia served before me, taking over from a distant cousin who abandoned the post long ago. I was a child when she died and the court seers declared that either Maxaltic or I would take up her mantle. Two years ago, my abilities made themselves manifest. My brother hardly spoke to me afterwards—that is, until he asked for the Retelling."

Johnny emerged from the water, shifting into his normal self and wrapping himself in warm jeans, tennis shoes and a hoodie. "That's freaking amazing, Princess Anamacani, though it sucks your brother is being such a moron."

"Please, Juan, call me Ana."

He nodded, trying hard not to blush. "Cool. My name's actually *Juan Ángel* in Spanish. You should call me Johnny. It's English, but that's my nickname."

"As you prefer, Johnny." The "j" was almost a "sh" the way she said it.

Pulling his eyes away from her self-consciously, he looked around and finally noticed the hundreds of scrolls and tomes arranged in niches and on stone shelves throughout the Cave of History. Illumination came from an almost steampunk collection of gaslights fed by copper tubing that Johnny guessed brought up volcanic gasses from deeper in the complex of caverns. Strange plants climbed walls and curled around stalagmites. Tables and chairs stood in disarray in various spots, covered with parchment, vellum and writing utensils.

"Whoa. My dad would flip if he saw all this. You guys have your entire history in here? How far back does that go? A couple thousand years?"

Ana smiled and shook her head. "Come here. Let me show you."

They walked deep into the cave, past the gaslights. She lit a candle and made her way along a narrow ledge beside a bubbling sulfur spring. The scrolls gave way to clay tablets, then to slabs of stone.

"Here it is. The First Document. You named it in my parents' throne room. The Compact of Blessed Creatures, carved into this bit of granite 80,000 years ago."

Johnny peered at the strange hieroglyphs, unlike anything he'd ever seen in his father's books or in history class.

"Wow."

"Indeed. It is daunting, serving as the steward of all this knowledge, adding to it with my own quill."

"You, uh, do seem kind of young."

Ana laughed. "Yes, well, I have lived through but twenty-three years."

The chagrin must have shown on his face, because she laughed even harder.

"Ceremonial years, Johnny. Seventeen solar years. Why, how old are you?"

He found it tough to admit the truth, but did so anyway. "Hrm, thirteen."

Gesturing with her candle, she guided him back toward the brighter part of the cave. "You look older to me. Of course, I have seen very few humans, so it is difficult to judge. However, in a way, you are older than I am. The Atlacah live about twice as long as humans do, so in relative terms, I have lived less of my life than you."

They stopped at a table across which was spread a map of what appeared the entire Pacific Ocean. Five regions were marked and labeled in an odd script that reminded Johnny of Chinese or Japanese.

"So you guys have been around for 80,000 years, huh? Where did you come from?"

"From remarks you made in the throne room, I take it you know of Quetzalcoatl and Tezcatlipoca, correct?"

"Oh, yeah." His awkwardness faded. It was hard not to feel pride in his accomplishments, so Johnny didn't even bother with false humility. "I've spent some quality time with the Feathered Dude's animal soul, and I recently faced off against none other than Mr. Peg-legged Lord of Chaos himself, down in the bowels of Mictlan."

The look on Ana's face was priceless. Johnny had clearly gone up a dozen or so notches in respectability.

She swallowed heavily. "I see. Well, at the beginning of the Fourth Age of the world, the struggle between the brothers continued. A new sun was needed, but the gods wanted to avoid the disputes of the past. After a time they looked to Matlalcueyeh, the green-skirted goddess of water, wife of the rain god Tlaloc. Powerful enough to sustain the world yet sufficiently loving and gentle to care for her charges, Matlalcueyeh seemed an ideal candidate."

Johnny cleared his throat. "Uh, you don't actually mean that she became the sun, do you? That must be a metaphor or something."

"To be honest, I cannot claim to understand the ways of the gods. Our priests tell us that the brothers agreed on her as the right choice, and she was somehow transfigured, becoming the governing force of the world, controlling the sun and all else that sustains life. The men and women created by the gods had many children, and those had many more, and the earth began to fill up with human beings whose praise and sacrifice sustained the sun and pleased the gods.

"Much time passed in this way, it is said, idyllic and serene. Then the heavens began to fill with water. It is not clear precisely why or how, but our annals report that Matlalcueyeh wept for fifty-two years, her tears accumulating in the sky until it bowed with the weight of her sadness. The source of that weeping will be forever a mystery though circumstances suggest—"

Johnny smirked. "Let me guess. Tall, dark and smoky was to blame."

"As far as we can determine, yes. He was, at least, the only god aware of the danger, for he forewarned an aging couple, making them store food in a hollow log and seal themselves within. Then the firmament shuddered, cracked, and ripped wide open. The heavens fell, flooding the sea-ringed world till it seemed a part of the cosmic sea, obliterated from existence entirely. Most people drowned, but Quetzalcoatl, rushing into the breach, attempting to staunch the tide, transformed a small number of survivors into merfolk, doughty sirens and tritons who dove deep to avoid the pounding storm."

"Your ancestors."

"Not entirely. One strand of my heritage."

She looked down at her legs and wiggled her toes. The gesture appeared at first playful, but then Johnny realized she was avoiding his gaze.

"The real story of Tapachco begins after human beings arrive," she said, her voice dropping almost to a whisper, "when the first shapeshifting twins in history betray each other and all they love, nearly destroying the world afresh."

CHAPTER SIX

It was hard not to like and trust Mihuah. The twenty-something diplomat had dismissed all but two of her aids, insisting that she and Carol were perfectly capable of protecting themselves within the confines of the city. Once they were free of the entourage, she had offered to braid the human girl's hair, which kept floating in front of her eyes, before they set off. Mihuah's own tight rusty curls were closely cropped against her ochre skin and posed less of a challenge.

Their excursion had focused on major institutions, and Mihuah hadn't held back in sharing gossip about the royal family, priests, politicians and even troupes of actors. Much of this was delivered in a vicious deadpan that had Carol giggling despite herself.

"Below us you will see the largest collection of blowhards in the city," she said, toward the end of their tour of Tapachco. She indicated a broad structure with an ochre-freckled hand. "Well, it is empty at the moment, since the Assembly of Calpolehqueh is not in session. But a few weeks ago, the heads of every district were united there, trying their utmost to undo millennia of tradition and precedent on bullheaded whims."

"Sounds like our politicians. Only we have a lot more than you."

Mihuah shot her a look of feigned pity.

"You are welcome to remain in atlacatl form and avoid human politics in Tapachco, though I can't promise the boredom won't cause you greater distress. Ah! I spend a great deal of my time there," she said, gesturing at a spindly tower. "The Palace of Ministers, where the executive council lives and works. My mother, Aquimichin—who is the Queen's sister, by the way—is the Cihuacoatl, the minister of state. She is off visiting Unazoko now, so I am required to pick up quite a bit of slack. The deputy minister is awfully lazy, frankly."

Carol lifted a hand. "Hang on. That's a lot of information. Unazoko—another kingdom of merfolk?"

"Ah, apologies. Yes, a lovely, diverting city-state near your country of Japan. It is one of the Five Nations spread throughout the Pacific. We have lived in peace for several hundred years, thankfully. Of course, there are many other threats to our existence, the largest of which is humanity, no offense."

"None taken. We're definitely a menace, even to ourselves. How do you do it, though? Keep your existence a secret from us, I mean."

"We have nowhere near as much magic as the Little People, but we do have a smidge. Enough to help us withstand even the crushing pressures of the Deep, for example. And you have already encountered our tzaccayotl, the glamor we use to disguise ourselves as other marine creatures. This is merely an illusion laid over our true forms, but it is normally enough. The danger of capture is real, so if we die beyond the borders of the realm, our bodies dissolve into nothing within an hour."

"Yikes. But, uh, I'm guessing that stuff happens sometimes,

no? I mean, you guys show up in myths across the globe, and I just met a whole family that used to work with merfolk."

"Well, yes, of course. We have had official dealings with humans down the years, but the few of your kind who have betrayed our trust have been easily discredited in the eyes of their people. In addition, many guards and laws are in place to govern our behavior out in the open sea, though rogues will be rogues. As a measure of last defense, the court sorcerers are capable of influencing the weather around these isles and touching the minds of men to turn them away from deeper nearby exploration."

"Ah, I can see why diplomacy is so important. The Five Nations pretty much need to stick together, no, to keep humans out of Atlacah affairs? No wonder the Queen was so upset about Maxaltic dumping his would-be bride."

Mihuah's lip quivered, and she turned her face away.

Uh-oh, thought Carol. *I just hit a nerve.*

"It was not the first time he had done so," the diplomat muttered, choking back emotion.

"Oh, gosh, I'm so sorry. I should just keep my big mouth shut."

Mihuah ran a hand across her tight curls, straightened her elegant yoke, and turned to face Carol with a wistful smile. "Oh, it is hardly your fault. I was betrothed to Maxaltic as a young girl, an arrangement between our families. He is a few solar years older, you understand. I grew up quite enamored of him, but he was a distant, almost legendary figure. Anamacani was born, and I often spent time with her. We would be sisters-in-law one day, after all, not only cousins. Our bond grew strong."

Mihuah looked off into the distance wistfully. Carol wished she hadn't said anything. It was always uncomfortable, listening to the romantic tragedies of strangers. But she kept quiet and waited.

"When the Queen decided that the realm was better served by political ties to Qucha Llaqta, she had the prince tell me in person. It was the first and last time we spoke in private. He was kind. But I was nonetheless devastated."

Carol was just about to ask the diplomat whether she had ever traveled with her mother to that kingdom when a high-ranking guard swam up, accompanied by a young siren.

"Captain Xicol," Mihuah said in acknowledgment. "Where is the princess?"

The siren spoke up first, gripping her hands to a chest in a merfolk curtsy. "My Lady, Princess Anamacani has sent us to bring you to the Cave of History. She wishes to meet with you and Lady Carol."

"Just Carol, please. We're not royalty or anything like that."

Mihuah gestured to her aids. "We will be accompanying Ilancueh and the captain. Please report our whereabouts to the Royal Guard."

Thankful for the reprieve from the awkward conversation, Carol marveled at the traffic moving back and forth from the distant cave complex. As they approached and entered, she was amazed at the extent of agriculture and animal husbandry.

I guess these are all the little details that get left out of the fairy tales. A day in the life of a mermaid. I wonder how long it'll take Johnny to ask them about underwater toilets or something completely inappropriate like that.

They finally reached a vast cavern illuminated by a glowing circle of light above them. "The entrance to the Cave of History," Mihuah explained. "It is full of air at approximately the same pressure as you normally breathe. You will be able to assume your human form if you wish."

Moments later, Carol's head broke the surface in the cave. The Atlacah had lungs as well as gills, and her shifted body automatically made the change to respiration.

Blinking her eyes, she adjusted to the gaslight and saw her brother, standing at a table beside a human girl in her late teens.

"The real story of Tapachco begins after human beings arrive," the girl was saying softly, "when the first shapeshifting twins in history betray each other and all they love, nearly destroying the world afresh."

Turning to check on Mihuah—who was gripping a boulder and panting lightly—Carol hauled herself up onto the rocks, shifting and twisting the Robe of Mayahuel into pants, sweater and boots to stave off the cold, stale air.

"Uh, hello, there."

Johnny turned. "Hey, Carol," he said in Spanish. "Ana was just sharing the history of her people with me."

"Ana?"

"Yeah, you know, Princess Anamacani? She's an Air Sage, like a mermaid nagual with a human-shaped tonal."

"Oh!" Carol recovered and stuck out her hand. "Nice to meet you again, Ana."

The Tapachcan princess looked at the proffered palm and took it between both her own for a moment. "Likewise, Carol. We were discussing the origin of the Atlacah. I was telling your brother how, at the end of the Fourth Age, Matlalcueyeh's tears flooded the world, but—"

"Sure, I know the story from Aztec sources. But isn't she called Chalchiuhtlicue?"

"By some, yes. That is the title the Mexica gave the goddess. 'Her Skirt is Jade.' They did so love that precious stone."

"When I arrived, I heard you talking about the first pair of shapeshifting twins and how they almost destroyed the world. What's that all about? How does it connect to your people?"

Ana fiddled for a moment with one of her dreadlocks, which were dark brown now instead of their normal blue. "It is a difficult tale to tell, but one we all should keep in mind, even my cousin there…"

Mihuah waved affably. "I am listening, albeit with smaller ears than the three of you."

Hey, not bad! Johnny thought. *Not as funny as me, but it's tough to reach this level of comedic perfection.*

You keep telling yourself that, Mr. Stand-up.

"This is the same bit of history that my brother requested in the formal Retelling I did for him, though I will keep it straightforward, skipping unnecessary details," Ana said.

For your benefit, I'm betting, Carol quipped.

Ah, now who's the joker?

Ana rounded the table to stand between the twins and her cousin. "Thousands of years before recorded history, a great empire called Atlan arose on an island continent in the Pacific."

"Atlantis!" exclaimed Johnny. "Dude, I knew it."

"It *is* probably the source of those legends, Johnny. Now, Atlan was fabled for its seven cities, each cradled in one of the island's extinct volcanoes. For centuries, these were independent nations, often in conflict with one another, ruled by mighty women and men who wielded almost godlike powers. Many of them were shapeshifters.

"One day twins were born into the royal family of the kingdom of Sulamala: Epan Napotza and his sister Quelel Huetzo. With time, it became clear that these two had access to abilities well beyond those of even the greatest of humans. *Savage magic*, the sorcerers named it, trying to train the royal twins as best they could to channel their power for the good of Sulamala."

This is really creepy, Carol thought at her brother. *She could be describing us.*

Yup. Especially the whole "godlike" part. I'm kind of an Adonis, if you hadn't noticed.

Oh, shut up, weirdo. You're just all chiveado *because of the attention she's been giving you.*

What? Dude, I so knew you were going to start with that crap…

Ana continued, unaware of the exchange. "As a young man, Epan Napotza used his abilities to explore the ocean around Atlan, and there in the depths he discovered the merfolk. Living among them for a time, he fell in love with the siren Mrisu."

See? She's giving you hints, Johnny.

Hey! Not cool, Carol.

"His sister eventually found him, frantic with the news that their father had fallen deathly ill. Upon their return, even though Epan Napotza had abandoned his place in the kingdom for years, the dying king chose his son as his successor. Quelel Huetzo, secretly furious and bitter at not getting the crown though she had stood by her father's side always, cloistered herself away from the world."

Carol swallowed heavily. The story was full of frightening implications. She saw Johnny wince a bit, his usual bravado faltering.

"Once king, Epan arranged to marry Mrisu, and their union solidified an alliance between his kingdom and the Atlacah. The siren princess bore him seven sons, and when they had grown to manhood, they helped their father and their merfolk allies to conquer with very little bloodshed the other six cities. Thus was Atlan forged in those early days of the Fifth Age, long before what your people call recorded history."

She gestured at the extensive library around her with an ironic twist of the head.

"But what about the sister?" Carol asked. "Quelel?"

Ana looked away for a moment. Mihuah grimaced as if she knew what was coming.

"After decades alone and embittered in her woodland demesne at the heart of the island, living as a beast for years at a stretch, Quelel Huetzo was visited and seduced by Kisin, Lord of Xibalba."

"Yes, we know that creep," Carol cut in with a shiver. "He sliced our chests open and tried to eat our hearts."

"Major jerk," Johnny agreed vehemently.

"Kisin promised Quelel revenge against her brother the emperor, speaking of an instrument of destruction that would tear down all the Epan had constructed without her. You see, when the creator gods first formed the earth from the flesh of the primordial reptile, the reptile bit off one of Tezcatlipoca's feet, swallowing it whole. But the foot was never fully digested. A ball of ambergris built up around one of the bones—the other bones being expelled into the cosmos. This black sphere became known as the Cehuallocozcatl or Shadow Stone, and it rested at the heart of Mictlan for ages."

"Oh, snap." Johnny shoved his hands into the pockets of his hoodie. "Atlan was destroyed by the Shadow Stone. You don't mean..."

"Yes. Quelel used a *chay abah* to enter Mictlan. There, with Kisin's aid, she retrieved the Shadow Stone. An army of demons at her back, she emerged from the Land of the Dead and wielded that tool of darkness against her brother and his soldiers. But she won no victory. Instead, the entire island was shattered and sank beneath the waves."

A tinge of sad premonition made Carol's stomach flop. "Oh, my God. Tell me some people survived."

"Yes. A handful of humans escaped the cataclysm, heading for the distant coast of North America. These are some of the ancestors of the indigenous peoples of your continent, who intermingled with other humans crossing from Asia tens of thousands of years later. Among these were members of the royalty, some of whom passed down the ability to shapeshift to their children."

"Whoa," exclaimed Johnny. "So that's where natural-born naguales come from, where me and Carol come from."

Ana nodded. "Yes. Also, some of the emperor's sons and grandchildren, being half-Atlacah, were able to transform and flee the devastation with Mrisu's people, whose own underwater kingdom was also destroyed in the cataclysm. This group of refugees made their way north and west to found the Five Nations."

Carol narrowed her eyes a bit. "So some of the descendants of Epan are, what do you call yourselves? Air Sages."

Mihuah finally spoke up. "Exactly. From the House of Napotza, like Ana here, or our late Aunt Omelia and her cousin Celic."

Johnny perked up. "Celic? We know that name. He's the guy who told the Little People about your brother's plans."

Both Ana and Mihuah appeared stunned. The princess finally spoke. "That is difficult to believe, my friends. Celic abandoned his position as Royal Historian to join the Order of the Deep. As far as anyone knows, he lives in monastic seclusion far south of Tapachco."

"Ana, we *know* the Little People. They wouldn't lie about this."

Mihuah looked pleadingly at the princess. "Cousin, perhaps we should not let your mother hear the source of the news. We both know that she is probably doing all she can to obstruct any offensive against Maxaltic."

Carol raised her hand. "Hang on—what? You don't think your mother wants to stop her son from causing the apocalypse?"

Ana shook her head. "No, you misunderstand. I know my mother well. Maxaltic is certainly her favorite, and she will do everything she can to support and protect him short of allowing him to trigger a deluge. Yet that is not my chief concern. For years the Queen has pushed the court sorcerers to recreate ancient rites and spells. I worry she will attempt to recover the Shadow Stone for herself."

Johnny rubbed his hand across his face. "That's crazy. What would she do that for? Does *she* want to flood the world, too?"

"No. Of course not. But Mother's unification project has ground to a halt, and an object of such power would ensure the primacy of our house, of Tapachco, of Atlacah in general."

Carol sighed. "So, politics."

Mihuah gave a weak laugh. "Indeed, Carol. At the expense of anything, including a siren's heart."

At that moment, everyone was startled by a pair of flailing arms that broke the surface of the water. Mihuah reached out and steadied the sputtering form of Ilancueh.

"Your Royal Highness," she managed to say in Nahuatl. "Her Majesty Queen Iztalli has summoned you and the visiting dignitaries to the throne room."

"Uh, we're not really dignitaries," Johnny pointed out.

Yeah, you clearly have no dignity most of the time, so it's definitely a tough sell.

Ha! I'm really rubbing off on you, aren't I? Well, time to high-tail it out of here. Get it? High-tail?

Carol shook her head in feigned disgust and dove into the sea.

<hr>

C arol and Johnny were grilled for the better part of an hour by the Queen, the King and their various ministers. When the name of Celic came up, the twins were escorted out of the chambers for nearly another hour. Toward the end of their wait, Johnny shook his head vigorously.

"Okay, let me make sure I've got this straight. Tezcat's toe becomes the Shadow Stone. Crazy shapeshifting twin uses it to attack her brother and accidentally sinks Atlan. The thing is lost.

Fast forward 80,000 years. Malted Milkshake decides he also hates everybody, probably with a nudge from Tezcat. He runs off, puts together an army of monsters, starts to search for it. Right so far?"

"Yup." Carol knew what he was doing, taking all the information they'd been bombarded with and trying to boil it down to the core issue. Their mother operated the same way. "And now the question is—what do we do about it?"

As if on cue, they were called back before the council and the sovereigns. King Nextic floated free of his throne, moving closer to the twins. Mihuah and Ana swam to their sides as well.

"I have reached a decision," the King announced.

Yeah, right, Johnny quipped. *You mean the Queen has told you what decision to reach.*

Hush. Behind every great man, Johnny. Just think of Mom and Dad.

"Even were I so inclined, no formal military action can be taken against my son unless approved by the Assembly of Calpolehqueh. I have requested a special session, but there is work to be done first. None of us in this city knows the present location of Maxaltic. In order to take the appropriate action in its due time, we must remedy this ignorance.

"You two will travel with Castellan Nalquiza to the cloister of the Order of the Deep, escorted by a phalanx of guards for defense. Also in your company will be Lady Mihuah from the diplomatic corps and, much to my dismay, Princess Anamacani. Together you will question Brother Celic and conduct whatever further investigation is necessary to learn the whereabouts of the prince."

"Thus will we also verify the truthfulness of the accusations that you claim the tzapame have made," the Queen added coldly. "And in the event that your arrival is part of some plot against Tapachco, rather than what you have told us, the chief sorcerer of the court, Archmage Tenamic, will be joining your party when it departs in the morning."

Figures. Look at the Queen's smug face, Johnny remarked. *She's more interested in the location of the stone. The sirens were right on the money about her.*

Well, Ana and Mihuah might be pretty suspicious of the Queen's motives, but searching for the Shadow Stone actually makes the most sense. Nobody even knows where Maxaltic is, but I'm guessing somebody can lead us to what's left of Atlan. I wonder why they don't just come out and say that.

What's that phrase they always use in the movies? "Plausible deniability." This way they can, you know, blame everything on Nalquiza or us if stuff goes south.

Then we've got to make sure it doesn't.

"Okay, Your Majesties," she said, as self-assuredly as she could manage. "Though we wish you had more faith in us, count us in."

CHAPTER SEVEN

To Johnny's relief, dinner was announced not long afterward. All the swimming, plotting and planning had left him really hungry, and he was also very curious to see how a meal could be served under water without everything just floating away.

The dining hall was dominated, not by a table, but by a ring of strange yoke-like contraptions. As guests were ushered in, they were led to these stations in some predetermined order. Johnny was directed to the one beside Princess Anamacani, and she showed him how to properly slip himself into the loops of sanded coral so that he could rest without drifting off.

"This is super different from the way humans do things," he remarked.

"It is indeed. I have yet to eat in human form, but you sit at tables, do you not?"

"Yeah. You're going to have to talk me through this, because I've barely got a clue about how to eat right in the human world, much less in a royal dining room in an underwater kingdom."

Ana laughed lightly. "Of course. Rest easy, friend."

Across the circle from them were Mihuah and Carol, probably having a similar conversation from the way the diplomat was guiding his sister into her nook and gesturing discretely at people around them. Conversation twittered and whistled steadily until the King and Queen finally arrived, settling into the largest, finest of the dining yokes toward the end of the chamber.

"Friends, family, subjects," Nextic called as everyone fell silent. "It is with heavy hearts that we gather to dine on the eve of a weighty expedition. Tapachco, mourning the apparent loss of its crown prince, mingles hope with grief; faced with the possibility of his return or his betrayal. For the first time in millennia we host human guests here in this kingdom beneath the waves, but we can scarcely bring ourselves to fete the bringers of such horrible tidings. So let us offer a prayer to the gods, to Quetzalcoatl and Tonantzin, to Matlalcueyeh and Huixtohcihuatl. May this food and this fellowship prepare us for whatever they will, may they perhaps deign to return Maxaltic back to us unharmed and whole, repentant and ready to resume his role. Yet, if their will be his destruction, let their wrath be wrought through the might of their champions."

Johnny figured the Queen didn't enjoy this little speech too much by the way she proceeded to ignore her husband throughout most of the meal.

"She really doesn't like us, huh? And this chief sorcerer? Tenamic? What's the deal with him? Point him out for me."

Ana shook her head. "No, he is absent this evening. Along with his acolytes and fellow mages, he has spent a fortnight attempting to divine Maxaltic's location through various incantations. They will be making one final attempt tonight."

"Well, that whole 'the chief sorcerer will deal with you if you're lying' monologue your mom gave was pretty uncool."

Ana touched his arm reassuringly. "No matter how it

sounds, no matter how cold and rude he may act toward you and Carol, I can assure you that Tenamic is one of the most ethical citizens of this realm. You have nothing to fear from him."

"Good to know. I sure hope you and Mihuah vouched for us with your parents, though. We're not trying any sneaky stuff, you know."

"We did, Johnny. My cousin and I are excellent judges of character, and we believe you and Carol to be truthful, sincere, and decent."

Soon a dozen attendants swam into the chamber, baring small coral globes that they distributed among the guests along with ornately carved utensils that resembled miniature harpoons. Ana explained to Johnny how to twist open the top of his globe and delicately spear the green spheres that rested within. He cautiously tasted one, then excitedly stabbed at the rest. It appeared to be some sort of spiced fish wrapped tightly in aquatic greens, and to his shifted tongue it was sheer delicacy.

"You may want to slow down," Ana said, repressing a laugh. "It's considered a little uncouth to eat with such zeal."

Grinning, he tried to be as sophisticated as possible, though, like he always told his mom when she scolded him for bad table manners, it really didn't make much sense. *Food is energy. Eat it quick and get on with doing stuff.*

Once they had cleared the spheres, the attendants next brought in carved crystal globes, holding them carefully upside down. Johnny grabbed his by the bone hand grip on the side after being warned that the dish was hot.

"Take care not to tip your bowl," Ana warned. "It is filled with heated air and a cooked mélange of shark, squid and greens.

The pressure keeps water from entering, but too much of a tilt will send the air bubbling out and cool the contents too quickly."

"Weird. It's like a reverse soup!"

Ana showed him how to use a pair of strange ivory tongs with bent tips to reach up into the bowl and grab food, pulling it down into the water and then up to his mouth. The stew was even better than the spiced-fish balls.

"Dang, I could really get used to this cuisine!"

There were a few more courses, including skewered shrimp and coral tubes from which everyone sucked a tartly sweet paste for dessert. The oddest thing for Johnny was the lack of drink. The merfolk were inhaling water through their noses, the same way they did when resting. When they moved, water rushed over their gills from the outside, so they never had to drink.

Really bizarre. Don't know what I'd do without a Coke every now and then.

Toward the middle of the meal, the night's entertainment began. The first performance was some strange aquatic dancing— ridiculously boring— followed by a pretty cool acting troupe that put on a short play about the love of a farming siren for a shark-herding triton. It was okay, Johnny figured, but it was full of merfolk allusions and jokes that he didn't get, though he smiled a lot at Ana's delighted laughter.

Once the event was over, he and Carol were escorted by Mihuah, Ana and a couple of guards to guest rooms in a lower level of the palace.

"Remember, Carol," he said when they reached the swiveling doors of their quarters. "Let your tonal take over completely before going to sleep."

Ana went inside with him to explain the use of the various hooks, baskets and other odd furniture in his room. There was a sort of weird toilet contraption in a small adjoining room, but an embarrassed Johnny just accessed his borrowed memories for details on how to use that.

"And there you have the sleeping alcove," the princess said, pointing out a recessed half-sphere of space on one wall. "The walls are covered in a soft material, and you just pull the entrance netting up onto these hooks so you avoid floating out into the room during the night."

"Awesome. Okay, then, I guess I'm going to get some shut-eye. Got to get up early, don't we?"

"Indeed. Rest well, Johnny."

She gave a sort of elegant curtsy. In a clumsy response, he brought two fingers up to his forehead to make the goofy salute that he and his father always gave each other, flicking his digits nonchalantly away from his brow.

"Uh, sure. Will do, Ana. You too."

The door rotated shut behind her, and he shook his head in irritation.

"That was really smooth, dude," he told himself. "Classy. What a moron."

Rather than think about how awkward he felt, he slipped into the alcove, called his tonal to the forefront of his being, and hid himself deeply in dreamless sleep.

Early the next morning, Johnny found himself forming up at the city's edge with Carolina, Mihuah, Castellan Nalquiza and a phalanx of troops that were loading up a team of sixgill sharks with equipment, guided by Captain Xicol.

"I'm really curious about the court sorcerer," Carol remarked.

"Yeah, me, too. Is he going to be more Dumbledore-slash-Ben Kenobi or Snape-slash-Dark Willow? Or a total oddball like Dr. Strange or Merlin?"

"You're a weird boy."

Before he could think up a clever comeback, a figure came swimming leisurely toward them. He was an old triton, Johnny could tell from the thin, frayed edges of his gills and tail, though age didn't weigh on the Atlacah as much as it did humans. Very dark gray with charcoal striping, the newcomer was completely bald, though his head, arms and torso were covered with a tight-fitting, black-scaled outfit that flared out into a type of kilt. He was otherwise unadorned, except for a jade disk hanging around his neck—engraved with a strange glyph—and a staff of ivory, ornately carved with other arcane symbols. His long, silver goatee was carefully braided, and his eyes were almost completely white, with just the black dots of the pupils peering at them as he approached.

I'm guessing this is Tenamic, Johnny thought to his sister. *Looks like he belongs in a Rob Zombie movie.*

Coming to a hovering halt before Ana, the sorcerer gripped his fists against his chest and inclined his head. "Good morning, Your Royal Highness. At your mother's behest, I arrive to accompany this expedition and to help it accomplish its charge."

"You are well come, Archmage Tenamic. Were your attempts

at finding my brother successful?"

"No, I am afraid they were not. Maxaltic is shielded by shadow magic, as far as I can tell. His whereabouts are beyond our power to determine."

"Then we'll have to track him down the old-fashioned way, huh?" Johnny quipped. "Using detective work and stuff."

The sorcerer raised an eyebrow. "You must be one of the naguales. Johnny, if I am not mistaken?"

"Yes, sir. That's me."

"It is a pleasure to meet you. And you are Carol, are you not?"

"Yes, um, Archmage Tenamic."

"Good, good. It is true that detecting is our only recourse, but the three of us will be able to bring some magic 'stuff' to bear on the mystery as well."

There was a twinkle in his otherwise scary eyes, and something told Johnny that, like Ana had said, they could trust the old wizard just fine.

"And we need to get started with this detecting immediately," the castellan said gruffly, gesturing at her phalanx of royal guards. "Captain Xicol, if you will lead the way."

The expedition set off in the direction of the caves, guards on all sides, the sharks with their packs toward the back.

And thus the Fellowship of the Shadow Stone set forth...

Stop. You're embarrassing yourself, Johnny.

What? I thought we could all cosplay. You can be Gimli the dwarf, Carol.

And you could be a towering troll, huh? Turned to stone?

You're no fun.

They began diving below the caverns dedicated to agriculture to enter a series of grottoes in which warmer water swirled with greater and greater force until they merged into a broad current that pulled the company along with increasing speed. Before long they found themselves rocketing out into the open depths of the sea through a broad opening in the roots of San Benedicto Island.

Riding the current was an unexpected relief, like getting into a car after walking several kilometers. Johnny smiled as he was carried along, twitching his tail from time to time to adjust his position alongside his sister.

"This is pretty sweet," he told her.

"Yeah. I wonder how long it'll last."

"Hopefully most of the way. You sleep okay?"

Carol shrugged. "I guess. I was nervous about drowning. Plus..."

"What?"

"Well, I couldn't stop thinking about Atlan and the first nagual twins, Johnny. How did they end up hating each other so much that they'd clash the way they did, causing so much destruction? I mean, I'm guessing that when they were our age, they had to be pretty good friends. Like, uh, you and me."

"I don't know, Carol. For, what was her name, Quelel to get so angry and jealous, her brother was probably a big jerk to her. Maybe their parents were a lot different, raised them not to see each other as equals, stuff like that. You know, all the macho stupidity you see in the world — like, boys are better than girls and so on."

"You're probably right. But I still worry. We can't end up like them, ever, Johnny. We have to talk to each other, share our concerns, our feelings."

"You bet, Sis. Besides, you know how I hate all that macho crap, anyway. This isn't a competition. We're in it together, to stop the bad guys and keep innocent people safe. I don't want to be king of anything."

Ana had overheard them and moved closer. "That is a noble sentiment, Johnny, though I suspect you would make a great leader. As would you, Carol. You should note, however, that the rage Quelel felt toward her brother was less driven by jealousy or rivalry than by disappointment at his abandoning their family, their ailing father, to spend so much time in the sea."

Johnny nodded. "Yeah, well, family means everything to me, so I can't see that happening. Besides, nowadays Epan could just talk to his old man every day using Skype, right, Carol?"

Mihuah had come along by this point, and Carol launched into an explanation of modern communication technology, mentally rolling her eyes at her brother.

Johnny took a moment to drop back a bit to where Tenamic traveled the current alongside Captain Xicol.

"So, gentlemen, about how far is it to the monastery?"

"About a quarter watch or so," the captain responded. Johnny did the math in his head—two hours. "Of course, that's depending on how quick we can move from this current to the Patlachtic Flow, which runs past the Order's cloister at the edge of the Acapulco Trench."

"Oh, sure, I know what that is. We crossed over the northern edge of it in a boat a couple of days ago. So, you guys use currents a lot for long-distance travel, do you?"

"Yes," the captain said. "Ahuecapan, the depths inhabited by the Atlacah, is vast, spread all over Apan, the Mother Ocean."

The Pacific, he means, thought Johnny as he nodded. "Sure, I can see how tough it'd be to visit the Five Nations on just tail power."

"Isn't this a problem in Atlixco, too?" asked the captain.

"I'm sorry, where?"

Tenamic gave a gentle laugh. "The Surface, Johnny. Thus do we name the world of humans and walking beasts."

"Oh, well, we use wind currents a little, 'walking beasts' some as well, but mostly we use technology to create vehicles that transport us from place to place."

Xicol grimaced a little. "Ah, yes, we've seen many of your ships, plying the sea or sinking beneath the waves to be reclaimed by coral and sea grass upon the ocean floor."

"Indeed," said the court sorcerer, "and to transition from there, I have learned that yesterday you gave our engineers and builders something of a show, Johnny."

"Oh, you mean making the coral grow faster? That was a shock for me, too."

"So you had never performed this feat before?"

"No. I saw the teotl in the coral and reached out with xoxal...It kind of just happened."

Tenamic stroked his beard thoughtfully, a movement that changed his balance and sent him into a slow spiral till he was essentially below Johnny, looking up at him. "Such abilities are not unknown to the mages of Tapachco. You have wielded *matlallotl.* Green Magic. With time—through great study and considerable practice—your mastery may allow you to bend the vegetable sphere to your every command."

Before they could continue with the conversation, Nalquiza indicated to everyone it was time to exit the current and drop into the massive Patlachtic Flow. Swimming in a spiral to reduce the shear, the company submerged into stiller, colder water. They traveled at top speed for five minutes before a saltier rush pulled at them and they were drawn into a sort of aquatic superhighway.

The group spread out even more, and the guards pulled rations from the pack sharks for everyone. As Johnny and Carol nibbled on their bits of fish, Mihuah compared the Flow to the much more impressive Black Stream, along which she had once traveled for weeks with her mother to visit the distant kingdom of Unazoko.

Once the novelty of the new current had faded, Johnny drifted off by himself, reflecting on the new knowledge he'd gained from the Archmage, gingerly opening his senses to any energy from nearby plants. All about, the ocean teemed with strange life, some of it surrounding the company, as in the case of a huge cloud of bioluminescent microorganisms, which turned the Flow into a glowing stream of blue for the better part of an hour.

The lightshow had begun to disperse when the castellan signaled that it was time to exit. She led the company west and down, the sea growing dimmer and dimmer. Tenamic rumbled an esoteric incantation, and the sorcerer's staff started to glow, lessening the gloom a little.

Soon, a shape began to loom in the distance. The phalanx quickened its pace at Captain Xicol's command, and they herded the younger members of the company toward a structure that seemed to coalesce out of the inky depths, lit up here and there by what might have been magic or bioluminescence.

It was the massive hulk of a sunken ship, lying on its starboard side, thickly coated with coral and other organisms. As they approached, Johnny realized it was perched on an outcropping that jutted out over the blackest abyss he could have imagined.

"Behold," Archmage Tenamic announced, "*Iztac Teopixcacalli*: the salt-scoured monastery of the Order of the Deep."

CHAPTER EIGHT

C arol figured the ship had sunk about a century ago, judging from the living crust that had grown over its hull. An armored corvette, probably. Sixty meters long, hints of rust among the coral, three masts lying half-buried in the sand of the ocean floor. Mihuah had suggested that the Order was thousands of years old, so this was either a recent branch or the monks had relocated from a previous monastery.

An entrance had been fashioned where the main mast had once stood. As the company approached, a group of tritons emerged with shorn heads. They were wearing simple loincloths, and large ivory medallions that were carved with the image of a siren, strapped by harnesses to their chests. Carol assumed the siren was Huixtocihuatl, the goddess of salt. Mihuah had mentioned that the Order was devoted to that divinity.

One of the monks, whose eyes were the same spooky white as Tenamic's, swam ahead of the rest to greet the newcomers.

The boss monk, Johnny thought at her.

Yeah. She was delighted to realize she knew the Nahuatl term for his position. *The* teopixcahuah. *Abbot, in English. Head of the monastery.*

Like I said. Boss monk. The image of a smiley face popped into her head.

Did you just use telepathy to send me an emoji? You're one...

...strange boy. Yeah, I know.

"Castellan Nalquiza. Archmage Tenamic." The monk made no gesture of respect, just inclined his head slightly. "It has been scores of years since I last beheld such lofty personages. You will pardon my lack of refinement in greeting you. A lifetime of silence and solitude, serving the goddess and watching the deep, efface such niceties."

"Abbot Pacqui," the castellan said, "we require nothing but information and rest."

"Ah," replied the abbot, a smile easing his stiff demeanor. "Those we can supply, I trust. Please, follow me."

Leaving a contingent of guards to keep watch and care for the sixgill sharks, the group swam into the heart of the monastery. The various holds remained largely intact, though the monks had used the decades to guide coral into the typical half-sphere cubicles and resting yokes that Carol had seen throughout Tapachco. The abbot led them into the largest of the holds, which had been converted into an assembly room. The walls were dotted with rings through which the monks hooked their tails, assuming a prayerful, bowed stance.

Like pews, she sent her brother as she followed suit.

N'hombre, don't remind me of the kneelers at St. Joseph's. Ugh.

Once everyone was settled, Nalquiza deferred to Princess Anamacani to explain the reason for their visit.

"Word may have reached you," she said, "of the disappearance of my brother, Prince Maxaltic, nine *veintenas* ago. Despite the efforts of the royal guard and the city mages, we had no idea where he had gone or why. Until the arrival of two human naguales, Carol and Johnny Garza, whom you see before you."

The abbot gave them a deeper bow of the head than he had his own countrymen, clearly surprised at their identities.

"The twins are here at the behest of the tzapame, who claim that Maxaltic seeks the Shadow Stone, accompanied by an army of dark beings."

One of the monks gasped involuntarily at this news. Abbot Pacqui shot him a silencing look.

"The Little People appear to have learned this information from Celic of the House of Napotza. Knowing that he is a brother of the Order, we have travelled here to question him further about his claims. Can he be quickly summoned? Much depends on the knowledge he may possess."

Pacqui shook his head. "I am afraid that is impossible, Your Royal Highness. Celic left us many years ago, abandoning the sea to become an *atenhuatl*."

There was stunned silence.

Carol ventured the question before Johnny could comment. "I'm sorry, but what's an atenhuatl?"

"River-dwellers," the abbot explained. "Air Sages who exile themselves to the Surface to live among humans and walking beasts, retiring to the unsalted and sickly sweet flowing waters of your realm when the need for their natural form arises. In ages past, when your people and ours had greater commerce, an atenhuatl would serve as a type of ambassador and priestly guide, communing with atlacah, humans, elementals and even gods. Those, of course, were very different times."

Sounds like Ariel from The Little Mermaid, Johnny quipped mentally.

"But," Carol continued, "if Celic's been living in Mexico or something for years now, how could he possibly know what's going on with Maxaltic?"

The abbot made a despairing gesture. "I have no idea, Lady Carol. For some time before his departure, Brother Celic had withdrawn from others of the Order, spending his days in isolated meditation. What prompted his decision to leave us is a mystery. He would not explain himself, and we do not force our members to remain if they choose to abandon their devotion to the goddess."

The castellan was visibly distraught, the scar on her face more livid than usual. "And Maxaltic? Have you had any news of him? Has he passed this way?"

"I am afraid we know nothing of the prince's whereabouts. None has reported seeing him or any signs of this dark army of his."

Some confused conversation began, with Mihuah and Ana heatedly arguing with the castellan and Captain Xicol. Tenamic made a slashing gesture with his staff and that silenced them.

"Very well. Let us do a bit of the 'detecting' that Johnny has suggested. Maxaltic appears to seek the Shadow Stone. What can the Order of the Deep tell us about that deadly device? What does your lore suggest? What might be its resting place?"

The abbot made a doubtful gesture with his hands. "We have no particular traditions concerning the Shadow Stone. As far as we know, it lies still in sunken Atlan, amid the ruins of Sulamala, gripped, no doubt, by the skeletal hands of the woman who last wielded its dire might."

Mihuah slipped from her prayer ring and floated closer to the monk. "And where *is* Atlan, Abbot Pacqui? If we got there before

Maxaltic, we could foil his disturbing plans."

"You will have to forgive us, Lady Mihuah, but its location was lost long ago. Perhaps the Royal Historian might know."

He gave a pointed look at Ana, who shook her head. "I am afraid not. Any maps or other guidance to the site were expunged tens of thousands of years ago from the Royal History."

The Archmage rested his bearded chin atop his staff thoughtfully. "There is a single mention of the ruins in the *Jade Grimoire*, the compendium of Tapachco's magic: 'Southeast lies that shattered land — at the very nadir of the Abyss.' And, indeed, it goes on to warn strongly against ever venturing close."

Captain Xicol's voice shook a bit as he spoke. "As a youngster, I heard stories of that place from my mother. Haunted by ghosts and demons, she warned, swirling up from Amictlan."

Johnny perked up at this word. "Is that like Mictlan? Because Carol and I saw tons of ancient ruins in the Underworld."

"It is possible an entrance to that realm can be found there, but Amictlan is what we call the Abyss, the lowest point of the Acapulco Trench. Even if the *Jade Grimoire* can be trusted, no living siren or triton knows the precise coordinates of that darkest of dark places."

Abbot Pacqui bent his head as if to pray. "And those stories the captain mentions are not simply told to frighten children, brothers and sisters. The Order of the Deep has encountered fell beings those few times we have ventured south along the trench. Along with kings and queens, we have therefore sought to dissuade merfolk from traveling this way toward the Abyss."

His fingers absently traced the form of Huixtohcihuatl on his chest. Then he suddenly twitched and looked up, his eyes wide.

"And yet..."

Everyone stared at him, waiting.

Uncurling from his ring, he signaled for the other monks and addressed the company. "You will please excuse us. I must consult the goddess. If you remain for a time, I may be able to provide some small sliver of aid. In the meantime, acolytes will attend to your needs for food and rest."

He spun and rushed with uncharacteristic haste through a rectangular slot that must have once been a door.

Carol looked first at the princess and then the castellan. "So what do we do now?"

"Now," said Nalquiza, "we wait. I will send back messengers to the Queen and King with detailed news about these setbacks. It will take them twice as long to return, so I do not anticipate a response for another watch. Gods willing, the abbot will have gleaned whatever knowledge he can by then. Armed with that and guided by royal commands, we will make whatever move seems best."

⬤⬤⬤⬤⬤⬤⬤⬤

After a simple meal of greens and squid, members of the company were assigned to empty cells; small cabins that still contained a few broken or tarnished artifacts from the humans who had once used them. Carol rested for a while before emerging to look for the others. She found Johnny outside the monastery, playing patolli with guards using weighted pieces.

"Hey, Carol," he called. "Want to come get your butt kicked by your brother in an ancient board game?"

"Uh, no, I'll pass. You seen Mihuah anywhere?"

"Said she was going to explore the area. These guys wanted to send someone with her, but she refused an escort."

"That's pretty much the way she is. Very independent."

She watched as Johnny rolled the beans, a slower action than it would be on dry land, and moved his pieces with a triumphant shout.

"Boom!" he said to the young guard across from him. "Three times in a row! Bow before my mad skills, Enehnel."

The warrior smirked. "You're definitely mad, boy. I'm guessing your spate of wins comes more from luck than skill, though."

"Yeah, yeah. Sore loser."

"Here's an idea, shapeshifter—why don't you hunt up a mollusk and transform into something that keeps its mouth shut?"

Carol rolled her eyes. *Found someone as snarky as you, huh?*

Me and Enehnel are cuates, *yo. Even if he doesn't know it yet.*

"I hate to interrupt this witty banter, but I had hoped to speak to you two, Johnny and Carol."

Archmage Tenamic had approached undetected, and he now gestured at the bulk of the main mast. The twins followed him to its midpoint, using a massive naval gun half-buried in the sand to anchor themselves.

"So, what's wrong?" Carol asked.

"Nothing in particular. Yet it seems wise to broach the subject of savage magic. From what I hear, you wielded it in Mictlan a few times, but understand that there were no living, sentient beings on hand, no potential accidental casualties."

"Xolotl warned us that no one could really teach us how to use it. That not even the gods know how."

89

"And I would not dare contradict the nagual of Quetzalcoatl himself. Nevertheless, though we may know little of the actual mechanism of savage magic, we grasp the powers it has granted its users."

A hint of movement drew Carol's eye. Princess Anamacani was emerging from the monastery. Catching sight of them, she swam in their direction.

"Savage magic seems to manifest more weakly," Tenamic continued, "in identical nagual twins. Most have been brothers—Hunahpu and Xbalanque, Monster-Slayer and Born-for-Water, Keri and Kame. But there have been sister pairs as well, notably Taiwo and Kehinde, who merged into a single being before leaving the living world."

Ana had reached them by this point and anchored herself close to Johnny. Carol refrained from dropping a teasing remark into her brother's mind.

"*Cocoah*—fraternal nagual twins, especially male-female pairs—are the ones whose abilities inspired true awe. Some could travel from place to place in an instant; others could command the very elements, raining fire and flood down on their enemies; while others learned to reach into the minds of their fellow humans and bend them to their will."

"It is written," Ana added, "that Manqu Qhapaq and his sister Mama Uqllu were able to grant others the ability to shapeshift with the touch of their hands. There are even obscure references to the power to undo death and create life where there was none."

"Correct," the sorcerer agreed. "The greatest of the nagual twins became *Texoxqueh*, Savage Mages, virtual gods on earth."

Johnny gave a wry laugh. "Yeah, well, being a Savage Mage didn't help Epan, did it?"

Tenamic's face grew somber. "No, Johnny, it did not. Just as we know some of the powers your predecessors wielded, we also have records of the impact they had on the world."

"Like what happened to Atlan?" Carol suggested.

"Indeed. The very first naguales of this Fifth Age poured their might into their conflict, which heightened the destructive potential of the Shadow Stone and put the world in peril. But they were not the last."

"Archmage," Ana warned, lifting her hand.

"You would have me keep this knowledge from them?"

Carol felt her heart lurch with painful premonition.

Johnny got very serious very fast. "What? Keep what from us?"

The princess reached out and touched his arm. "Nothing, really. Please feel no alarm. It is only that several sets of shapeshifting fraternal twins also skirted the darkness the way Epan and Quelel did. However, the world is different now, friends. You are different. And from what you have told us, Quetzalcoatl believes in you, trusts you."

"Right. He does. So we're not going to join the Dark Side, guys."

Carol glanced nervously at Johnny, remembering how he had almost lost control of his power in the Underworld.

"You may not need to," Tenamic said, voicing her deepest worries. "Undisciplined use of unbridled power could cause just as much destruction as deliberate evil acts."

Carol knew that he was right, that they should be more proactive about their destiny. "Please, Archmage Tenamic—anything at all you can do to teach or train us, to prepare us—we want to do this right."

"Of course. We can begin by talking about the powers you already possess. Mihuah tells me you dispelled Shadow Magic with song. You are a *teocuicani* or sacred singer. As fortune would have it, so am I. Specialized techniques exist for using *teocuicayotl*, sacred song magic. Different songs yield different levels of force, for example. The tune of our childhood are strong, but the ancient hymns mightier still. You will want to use the old songs of your people till you learn to compose your own."

"My father writes songs," she interjected. "I used one of his against the Shadow Magic."

"Excellent. You will likely master composition quickly. Let me teach you a simple merfolk lullaby so we can practice focusing your frequencies."

"Uh, I know I should probably hone my Green Magic, Carol, but while you prepare for *American Idol*, maybe Ana and I should go hunt up Mihuah. No matter how tough she thinks she is, it's dangerous to be just wandering off."

"Take Enehnel with you." *As a guard. And, uh, chaperon, too. Will you knock that off? Gah.*

After a few hours of practice, Carol found she could narrow the scope of her song to target small rocks, lifting or cracking them, depending on her frequency. Tenamic showed her strange aquatic scales that dipped in between the normal notes she was used to, and he instructed her on the best subjects for songs of persuasion, subdual, and shattering.

"Such would normally take even an adept student months to learn," he remarked as they headed into the monastery for the evening meal. "Quite impressive."

They joined Johnny and Ana, who had returned with Mihuah some time ago.

"This waiting is killing me," Johnny muttered around a mouthful of seaweed. "I want to get moving, deal with this loser already."

"We all grow impatient, Johnny," Mihuah said, "but diplomacy has taught me that most problems require time, reflection and long discussion to resolve."

"Yeah, I kind of doubt the diplomatic approach is going to do much good with Maxaltic, but hey, we can give it a try."

Ana appeared about to add something to this argument when the messengers rushed in.

"Where's Castellan Nalquiza?" asked the senior of the two. "We need to confer with her in private."

Captain Xicol led them away into the bowels of the ship.

Mihuah smirked. "I believe the Queen has some instructions for the castellan."

"Where are the reinforcements?" Ana seemed quite frustrated. "If we are to head my brother off or confront him, this small contingent of guards is hardly sufficient."

"Well, it's got to take time, no? Putting together their supplies, organizing them, etcetera?"

The princess relented. "True. I should be more trusting, but I have reasons for my doubts, friend."

A low, rumbly call made the water around them tremble.

"Vespers," Mihuah observed. "The monks will be coming in to make their evening prayers."

The twins and their young siren friends moved to the edge of the chamber and watched the members of the Order file in. Grasping one another's forearms, they arranged themselves in a sphere, chanting low and unintelligibly. Abbot Pacqui appeared and made his way to the center of the sphere. With strong, clear clicks and whistles, he intoned a prayer to the goddess:

> *Blessed Huixtocihuatl—*
> *When your brothers sought to harm you*
> *With a vast saline flood,*
> *You opened wide your arms to greet*
> *Your precious destiny,*
> *For salt is life, you understood.*
> *Coursing through our veins*
> *Our briny blood retains the charge*
> *Of heaven's sacred energy.*
> *And in the Deep, brackish flows*
> *Mingle dense and strong.*
> *From here all creatures did arise*
> *When the earth was young,*
> *And here we praise your noble name*
> *Until it meets its end.*

There was another wordless song, and the sphere dispersed. Castellan Nalquiza, followed by the scouts and Captain Xicol, entered the chamber.

"Abbot Pacqui," Nalquiza called. "The royal couple has sent me word. We are to journey toward the Abyss, to stop the prince by whatever means we must."

"Only to stop him?" Ana demanded. "There were no other instructions?"

Nalquiza paused for a moment. "Princess, I am not certain what you mean to intimate, but those are our orders."

Carol looked at the abbot. "Did you find whatever information you were looking for? Something that'll help us?"

He gave a tired nod. "As I have said, I know not where the Abyss lies. However, I do know where you can find an outcast *ahuah* with vast and ancient knowledge. The goddess has confirmed to me in a vision that this being is key to your reaching Atlan."

Carol remembered her father's photos. "An ahuah? A water elemental? One of the tlaloqueh?"

"At one time, yes. But this particular elemental was expelled ages ago from Tlalocan, that watery paradise to which atlacah souls travel upon death. Banished for some unknown wrong, it was condemned to abide here in the Deep."

Archmage Tenamic traced the runes of his staff with his webbed fingers. "Unpredictable and often dangerous beings, these tlaloqueh. We must be cautious in our approach. Understand that it is ancient and strange, a creature of water and magic from the depths of time. We cannot fathom its motives or predict its behavior."

"Then perhaps," opined Ana, "we should wait for the reinforcements my parents are no doubt sending our way."

"No," Nalquiza said. "There is no time. We will leave word here as to our destination. Get as much rest as you can, everyone. We leave in half a watch."

Four hours of sleep. Carol hoped it would be enough.

CHAPTER NINE

J ohnny hated getting up with anything less than eight hours' sleep—in fact, he preferred a good ten—but his adrenaline kicked in right away when Carol stirred him awake.

"I'm up, I'm up!" he assured her, untangling himself from the webbing the monks used to strap themselves still each night. "Let's go pump this elemental for info."

"Johnny, remember what Dad said—these things are like angels. They're the children of the rain god. Powerful beings."

"Yeah, I know, and this one might as well be a demon, since it got tossed out of the mermaid heaven or whatever. But we've kicked demon butt before, Sis. Just sayin'."

"Don't get too cocky, Johnny," she warned, but he was already swimming away, heading for the monastery entrance. He found the others forming up on the castellan's commands. The Archmage illuminated their preparations with his staff.

Ana greeted Johnny with a smile. "Three senior monks will be guiding us to the abode of the fallen ahuah, which is apparently carved into the wall of the trench some two thousand rods to the south. Castellan Nalquiza calculates that we should arrive in about three-quarters of a watch."

"Good. The faster we get there, the closer we'll be to stopping your brother."

Carol and Mihuah were the last to join them for a quick breakfast of tough seaweed rolls, and then the company set off at a challenging pace that left little energy for conversation.

From time to time, Johnny would refresh himself with savage magic, letting it roll over him from head to tip of tail, revitalizing his transformed flesh. He kept boredom at bay by reaching out to the various plants strung out below him and causing them to grow faster, to twine around each other, to pull themselves up by the roots and replant themselves elsewhere.

From time to time he caught snatches of his sister's humming and saw she was practicing as well, pushing and rolling and cracking stones as the group rushed along the trench's edge.

Getting pretty good at that.

Your magic isn't half-bad, either.

Yeah, I'm trying to make Tenamic green with envy. Get it? 'Green.'

Oh, lord, Johnny. You never change.

Except for getting taller, huh? That reminds me...I think I can help you grow another several centimeters once we're back on dry land, chaparrita.

Uh, no thanks. I'll let my DNA sort that out for me. Only need one giant in the family, anyway.

Aside from brief rest stops, the castellan drove them at an exhausting pace. When they finally halted for lunch, Johnny sidled over to Enehnel, who he'd discovered was pretty approachable. Coming from a family of agricultural workers, the guard was a lot less stuck up and distant than the more aristocratic members of the expedition, and Johnny enjoyed exchanging playful barbs with him.

"So I guess there's no time for a quick game of patolli, huh?"

"Not only that, Johnny—if the castellan saw us take the board out, she'd be so enraged magma would begin to dribble from her ears. When she's in this sort of mood, everyone knows to keep away and snap to without complaint."

"Well, I'm anxious to stop this joker Maxaltic, too, but she's pretty freaking intense."

"You've got to understand, boy, that her main job is keeping the royal family safe. Now, the prince not only left Tapachco from right under her nose—he also took a platoon of guards with him. So this is not just about obeying the King and Queen. She's got to redeem herself, you see. To set things right."

"Got it. I'll try not to annoy her. Too much, anyway."

There wasn't time for a lot of talk after that because the castellan soon whistled the command for departure, and it was back to the Olympic swimming.

Six hours into the trek, the monks indicated it was time to slip over the rim of the trench and approach the elemental's abode.

Johnny's eyes widened as he saw it—a complex and massive façade carved into the very rock, unlike anything human hands had ever crafted. There were strange twisting and tapering columns along a jutting and intricately carved semi-circular portico. Beyond this spiraling entrances had been set in a ring around a bas-relief image of a god with goggle eyes and vampire teeth. The structure was overgrown with pale green plants, but Johnny glimpsed through their vine-like leaves many strange runes, most suggesting themes of water, rain, salt and sacrifice.

"We have guided you hence," one of the monks announced

nervously, "but we will not remain. May the goddess keep and protect you forever."

With that, their temporary guides turned and swam away.

Archmage Tenamic regarded the façade with a sober expression. "An ancient temple of Tlaloc, god of rain and therefore all water, ruler of Tlalocan. He was sovereign of the world during the Third Age, which he destroyed in rage. We fear him, though our worship is directed at his consort, Matlalcueyeh."

"So this is like a kid getting kicked out of his house by his dad and then living in one of the family's previous houses with a big portrait of the old man hanging in the living room. Great. This elemental is pretty nuts."

Ana agreed. "We should be cautious and try to draw the ahuah out."

"And what if it refuses?" Mihuah asked. "Castellan Nalquiza, we should enter without delay. Why else have you driven us here with such haste?"

Carol looked like she was about to object, but the castellan unsheathed her long dagger and made a decisive gesture. "Lady Mihuah is right. The abbot assured us this creature would provide the information we require. Hesitation is unnecessary."

Not very diplomatic of your friend, there. Be ready for anything, Johnny warned.

Totally.

They swam between the dizzying columns into the portico, which curved up on either side into a bowl shape. Closer up, Johnny could make out bits of jade and emerald worked into the volcanic greenstone of the structure.

Fits with the weedy plants growing all over it, Johnny thought.

Then, as they reached the largest of the openings, those pale plants whipped out at the company, twining around them tightly. Johnny's first thought was to shapeshift, but his arms were pinned, so he couldn't get to his bracelet. He jerked his head up at Carol, who had bent her mouth to her necklace and was touching the tip of her tongue to a scale. With a glittering flash, she became a school of viperfish, slipping free of the trap easily and spreading out to start gnawing on the vines that trapped the rest.

Come one, Johnny, she cried into his mind. *Your Green Magic, dude!*

He closed his eyes and reached into the plants with savage magic. As he did so, he felt another presence leave them, alarmed by his intrusion. Johnny pulled at the vines, snapping them where Carol had weakened the stems.

A frond had wrapped itself around Ana's neck and was squeezing tighter. Tugging it away with a quick twist of his hand, he grew suddenly furious. Savage magic surged within him; he gave a snarling groan and tore all the plants away from the temple, sending them drifting off into the darkness below.

"We should've listened to Ana," he said to the rest, moving between them and the entrance as they checked themselves and their supplied. "We can't go in there. Who knows what kind of crazy traps are waiting?"

The viperfish swam toward him together and became Carol's siren form again. "He's right."

Tenamic drew near to the twins and raised his staff. Its glow intensified, causing strange shadows to dance on the rock. "O Lord of Water," he called. "Forgive our intrusion. We have come to pay our respects and beg a bit of wisdom. Pray, grant us a moment of your attention."

For a moment nothing happened, and Johnny prepared himself to ask in a much ruder way. But then a green iridescence shimmered in the dark interior of the temple, growing brighter and brighter until something at last emerged.

It was a translucent sphere, two meters in diameter. At its center Johnny could make out the source of the light—an emerald the size of his fist that radiated a steady green energy.

After bobbing before them for a few seconds, the sphere contracted and reshaped itself, taking on the form of an androgynous triton. Its "skin" grew slightly more opaque and textured, and the emerald's light shimmered hotly in the creature's goggle eyes and more transparent chest.

"Shapeshifting twins," it said in a voice that seemed to come from every direction, as if the sea itself were speaking. "Wielders of the savage magic that saves and damns. I had not thought to look upon your like again, you children of capricious fate."

"The surprise is mutual," Johnny quipped. "Though I'm kind of pissed you attacked my friends just now, Ms. Pseudopod. Or Mister, whatever."

"You may call me Xomalloh."

Carol came closer. "I'm Carol. My brother is Johnny. With us are—"

"None of them matter," the elemental declared, "except the mage." With a gesture like a conductor striking up an orchestra, it lifted a shimmering, blurry barrier that the castellan beat her fists against futilely.

The court sorcerer lowered his staff in deference. "I am Tenamic, Lord Xomalloh."

"As well you know, I am no Lord of Water. I am one of the Fatherless, stripped of authority, expelled from paradise."

"Still," Johnny said, "you're pretty powerful and you know a lot. We need directions, and at least one goddess suggested you could help."

The elemental appeared to think this over for a moment. "I see. It is unexpected that I should find favor with one of the Lofty. So be it. Ask me, mages."

Carol spoke without hesitation. "We need to get to Atlan, Xomalloh. Can you guide us somehow?"

It stretched out its arms, clutching fingers at the water, which coalesced into glowing weapons, a sword and spear that Johnny was willing to bet would cause serious damage despite being made out of liquid.

"What do you seek in that damned and broken domain?"

"It's not what we seek that's the problem, dude. It's what the army of monsters and psycho mermen are trying to recover. The Shadow Stone. And we've got to stop them. You get why, right?"

"How could I not comprehend?" The elemental's voice rang hollow with something like anguish. "I was there, human. One of the tlaloqueh tasked with guarding the civilization emerging on that island continent. When Quelel Huetzo strode from the bowels of Mictlan with that dark gem gripped grimly in her hands, we did nothing, convinced that the emperor, noble Epan Napotza, would reason with her, persuade her to turn away from that dire path. If he failed, had we not given unto his hands a mighty *nahualcuahuitl*, a sorcerer's staff carved from the very wood of the World Tree? Surely he would vanquish her, we believed, electing to remain impartial, as was the will of Quetzalcoatl concerning human affairs."

Carol reached out tentatively. Before Johnny could stop her, she had laid her hand on its glassy skin. Its weapons melted back into the water as she softly spoke. "But he didn't, did he? She wouldn't listen, and they were too equally matched."

A hint of black wormed around in Xomalloh's emerald heart for the briefest of seconds. "Even then some of us might have intervened, might have saved many lives. But I held my companions fast, halting their interference. We watched as Atlan sundered and sank in a cataclysm that rivaled the ending of an age. For this inaction were we expelled by our father Tlaloc, the Giver, the Green One. Therefore are we the Fatherless, and I the most reviled of our number here in the Deep."

Johnny tried to imagine the loneliness and despair, to be all alone with the weight of so much death and the memory of such rejection for tens of thousands of years.

"Gah," he muttered. "That really sucks, Xomalloh. And I know you don't want a repeat of it. So help us."

"Very well, human. Understand that the way is blocked for the Fatherless; not even our thoughts can contemplate the route to those ruins. But there was once a kingdom of tlacamichimeh here when ice clogged the seas, before your kind clambered from the savagery into which it had descended after Atlan's fall. Those man-fish raided the seven cities time and time again, and they built a series of waystations to guide and ease them on their piratical way. There is one nearby, a half-day's journey south, on the floor of the trench. Inside, you will find the knowledge you seek."

Tenamic gave a respectful salute. "We thank you, Xomalloh. Your aid will save many lives."

"May the gods wish it so, Mage. One thing is clear to me—the Shadow Stone has not been wielded. I know the taste of its bleak power. I would sense even here if anyone were to attempt its use."

The elemental slashed a limb through the dark water, and the barrier dissolved into nothing.

"Now, leave me to my fate, short-lived and fortunate fools. I no longer can bear the sight of others."

With that, Xomalloh collapsed back into its spherical shape and return to the cavernous darkness of the temple's interior.

Tenamic relayed the new information to Castellan Nalquiza, while Captain Xicol, Ana and Mihuah listened intently.

"And this explains a lot," Johnny said. "I'd been thinking, hmm, Maxaltic's got a huge head start on us, like six weeks or so. What if he already has the stone? But then I was also like—well, the massive flood hasn't started, yet, so maybe he hasn't found it yet."

Mihuah's eyes gleamed with understanding. "It must have taken him quite some time to gather his army; it seems reasonable that he is only now beginning to search for the stone."

"Good." The castellan rubbed her scar thoughtfully, adjusted the strap of her helm. "We can reach it before him. My scouts have found a suitable place for a camp—an escarpment a few dozen rods south. There we shall sleep for a half-watch before approaching the waystation. If we encounter resistance, we need to be well rested and ready."

The others were visibly relieved. Johnny nodded, but he wasn't sure he'd get much shut-eye. He was too pumped-up, itching for action.

Here we come, Maxaltic. Closer and closer, dude.

CHAPTER TEN

Carol watched her brother surge ahead, swimming between Enehnel and another guard. She was glad to see him looking up to the older tritons, even if his anxiousness to get into a battle worried her.

To divert her attention, she glanced at Archmage Tenamic, who swam a little above Mihuah and her, holding out his staff to illuminate the dark waters of the Deep.

"How does it work?"

The sorcerer turned his white eyes toward her. "My staff? Ah. To understand, you must first know that all Blessed Creatures—humans, merfolk, Little People, giants, and the rest—possess three souls. The everlasting part of us is our *teyolia*, our spirit, which lives on beyond our deaths, released into paradise and finally the unknown destiny that lies beyond even that."

Carol remembered the trials of Mictlan, and the role of the Underworld. For some humans, it stripped away their earthly connections so that the spirit could move Beyond, free of burdens, through that beautiful well whose music still haunted her dreams.

"You and your brother are intimately familiar with the second soul, the *tonalli*. At the moment of our birth, the teotl or divine energy of the universe begins to pour into us, infusing our blood and brains with a life force that resides both within us and without, subject to the whims of the gods who preside over our day signs, that astrological category into which we are born. In certain special individuals—Air Sages and naguales, for instance—this develops into a partly independent twin of our spirit."

"Like my tonal."

"Precisely. And the tonalli, given enough time—centuries, millennia—can acquire its own personality, as in the case of the gods."

"I see. That's why Xolotl and Quetzacoatl aren't exactly the same person."

"Yes. Even for the majority of people, the tonalli is a capricious and slippery thing, capable of leaving the body and traveling around. Moments of great stress, fear or surprise can send it scuttling like a wary fish. Such sudden absence leaves a person inexplicably ill."

Carol nodded. "In our culture, we call it *susto*. There are prayers and stuff to call the soul back, though I never realized that it was the tonal that was gone. What about the third one?"

"It is termed *ihiyotl*, the soul of emotions and passions, formed from sacred substances in the water or air that we breathe. We exhale streams of diluted ihiyotl from our lungs and gills. Most atlacah and human magic consists of manipulating these exhalations or the gases in our flesh. It is ihiyotl I draw upon and channel with my staff to light our way."

It was a more detailed explanation than Carol had expected, but it was helpful. "But savage magic doesn't use air-stuff, I don't think," she mused aloud. "I'm pretty sure it's teotl that we mess with, whether in the blood or in the air."

"I have no doubt. It is therefore dangerous and unpredictable."

Carol was about to retort when the Archmage slowed, scanning the sea around them and making his staff glow brighter.

"I sense something. Strange movement. Magical."

For a second Carol doubted him, then she felt it, too—a dark swirling, rushing at them from below.

"Everyone!" she shouted. "Something dangerous is coming!"

Then it was upon them, a massive whirlpool that glowed green as it seized the company and began to whip them about at neck-breaking speeds.

Shift, Johnny! We've got to save them!

She found the shriveled bit of calamari on her necklace just as the swirling reached her. Transformed into a monstrous squid, she anchored herself to the edge of the trench, wrapping a few tentacles tight around the deep-rooted rock.

Mihuah had been lifted high by the spinning currents and was now being hurtled toward the sea floor. Carol shot out a tentacle to seize her and drag her from the whirlpool; the diplomat went limp, blacking out from the extreme stresses on her body.

The Archmage was struggling to remain at the center of the vortex, streaming blue-white energy into it from his staff, clearly trying to slow the rotation of the current.

It was in vain. The whirlpool fed on his magic, growing even faster.

Carol flung her free tentacles out toward her other companions, yanking as many to safety as she could before they were dashed against the rocks or spun off into the black depths.

Johnny was shifting madly from one form to another, trying to find a way to help. In the form of a giant manta ray, he burst out of the spinning currents, rushing around it in a sort of orbit to catch guards flung outward.

The green of the vortex intensified and four massive water elementals coalesced from its violent eddies. With a burst of emerald lightning, one hurled her brother into the darkness.

Johnny! Carol screamed with all her mind.

One of the tlaloqueh materialized an enormous glowing club out of the dark water and smashed it violently against her. Reeling with pain, she lost her grip on her friends and slipped into unconsciousness.

She was back inside the temple at El Chanal. Her father was struggling in the water, which now reached his chest.

"Carolina, help me!"

Panic-stricken, she began to weep. "But how? We're trapped!"

"You'll have to destroy the temple, *amor*. Shift into something big, or use your sacred song magic to pulverize the stone."

The thought sickened her, paralyzed her. "No, wait, Dad. There's got to be another way. Let me—"

"There is no other way, you feeble pup."

Her father's eyes had gone glittering green.

"Tezcatlipoca." Pronouncing his name shattered the dream. The temple was gone. She was surrounded by a featureless expanse of darkness, tinged green like the underside of mottled leaves in deep shadow, broken only by the familiar shape of Ursa

Major, clinging tenuously to the gloom above.

Before her towered the Lord of Chaos, a smile playing across his pallid face. Behind his head hovered an obsidian mirror from which smoke uncurled in lazy, spiraling wreathes. He was dressed as he had been six months ago—a jaguar-skin cape flung across his shoulders, his divine flesh clothed in a gray tunic covered with dark feathers.

"Welcome to the Sixth Heaven, Carolina. My enduring abode. *Yayauhco*—Place of Eternal Dusk."

For a moment she couldn't find her voice. Then she rasped as mockingly as possible, "Heaven? More like another hell."

"Ah, indeed. You judge me with young, human eyes. You believe yourself to be good. Free of corruption. Selfless and heroic. But I see you, cur. You are a wolf at heart, and when the time comes, you will rip what you require from your enemies with the bloody teeth of your savage magic."

"No."

His cruel laugh would have melted the flesh from her bones had she been physically present before him. "Your refusal is irrelevant. Thus will you act, driven by your good intentions. In the end, like Quelel Huetzo, you will desecrate the world in the name of all you love."

"Never," she whispered, her chest crushed with dismay at his words. "You can't make me do it."

"I shall not lift a finger. You will choose destruction freely once my trials have prepared you. Now go. Behold what has been wrought upon your companions."

When Carol came to, she found Mihuah floating nearby. "She has awakened!" the diplomat called, and both Johnny and Tenamic rushed to her side.

"Are you okay?" her brother demanded, his face twisted with uncharacteristic anger. "That damn elemental gave you a serious *porrazo*, Sis."

"I'm okay. Had a vision of Tezcatlipoca, though."

"What?"

"The normal threats. Nothing to get worked up about. Is everyone okay?"

The Archmage regarded her with his zombie eyes. "No, sadly. We lost two guards, and—"

"Ana's gone, Carol. The elementals took her." Johnny's hands curled into fists. "And everybody's making excuses for why we're not going after them."

"It is madness, to begin with," Tenamic snapped. "Those were not the Fatherless, Johnny. They were true Lords of Water, scions of Tlaloc, wielding their full, divine might."

Castellan Nalquiza approached. Her glittering, fancy armor was scored and dented. A new gash had turned the scar on her face into an "X." "Lord Johnny, you must desist. Someone powerful is laying a trap for us. There are wounded. We lost pack sharks. I will *not* risk those under my command with limited supplies. I have sent my fastest messengers back to meet our reinforcements and relay my orders for utmost haste. We will wait until they arrive before pursuing the tlaloqueh."

"What if it's too late then? What if these freaking things are working with Maxaltic and he uses her to blackmail their parents? Look, me and Carol can deal with them, I know it."

"Deal with them?" scoffed the castellan. "As I recall, they dealt with both of you pretty handily just now."

"They caught us off guard! This time, we'll be the ones surprising them."

Stop it, Carol muttered telepathically, sending soothing sensations.

"Knock it off, Carol. You're not going to Jedi mind-trick me into compliance, dude."

"They're *gods*, Johnny."

"So what? Not even the gods have savage magic."

Tenamic shook his head disgustedly. "This arrogance is precisely what I warned the princess about. Damn the Little People for sending you, ill-prepared and easily manipulated by the Dark Lord. I wonder if we may have more to fear from the two of you than from Prince Maxaltic."

Carol blanched. "No, don't say that! Johnny just really cares about her—"

"Oh, and do we not, Lady Carol?" Nalquiza seemed close to weeping. "You have known her for two days. I saw her consecrated to Matlalcueyeh when she was a newborn. I have watched her grow into a revered young siren. Archmage Tenamic initiated her into the rites of the Air Sage. Lady Mihuah, her dearest cousin, nearly became her sister-in-law."

Mihuah sighed. "Please, let us not discuss broken betrothals right now. You need to consider another possibility, Johnny. Perhaps the elementals intend to distract us from our mission. What if Maxaltic is very close to reaching Atlan, and this kidnapping is meant to delay us long enough for him to find the Shadow Stone?"

Johnny put up his hand. "So, let me get this straight—you guys are super close to Ana and love her and stuff, but you're just going to sit here, wait for help, and maybe, if the broken-hearted diplomat over here gets her way, abandon the ROYAL HISTORIAN and AIR SAGE to whatever messed-up fate the elementals have in store for her? Wow. What a bunch of winners. Me? If my sister was taken captive? We wouldn't be talking. I'd be tracking those overgrown water bubbles down and popping them one by one."

That's enough. Really. They get it.

Pull yourself together, Carol. As soon as you're feeling better, we're going after her.

Wait, what?

You heard me. I mean, sensed my words or whatever. Look, more troops aren't going to make any difference, dude. We'd just have to save their butts again, and this time there'd even be more of them.

It was a point she hadn't considered. *Well...*

Xicol agrees with me, even if he's too respectful to contradict his boss. He can get some of the guards to come with, if that's the deal-breaker for you.

I don't know, Johnny. Let me think about it.

He sent a wave of annoyance and desperation, and sulked off to wedge himself under a boulder.

Enehnel brought her something to eat as the others continued to debate quietly. "Want me to try and talk some sense into the fool?"

"No. Thanks, but no. He just really hates injustice, hates seeing the innocent hurt. Give him some time to cool down. There is a logical side to him, deep down."

"Yeah, I've seen it when he plays patolli. He has strong strategy skills when he focuses."

Watching the wounded guards receive treatment, Carol chewed her food mechanically, knowing she needed the strength.

Tezcatlipoca's behind this. He's trying to manipulate us into doing something stupid. We've got to be cautious.

She turned her head to check on her brother.

He was gone.

CHAPTER ELEVEN

As much as Johnny loved his sister, she was still recovering from a major beating and a spiritual visit from the Lord of Chaos. Better to leave her behind. Besides, he had no intention of actually facing off against the stupid water elementals if he could help it. His plan was to use stealth and shifting to sneak past them and get Ana free. A huge army at his back would just screw things up.

The tlaloqueh left a pretty clear trail of energy—all Johnny had to do was give his tonal free rein, and he was off like a shot, deeper into the trench. Of course, without the glow of the Archmage's staff, he was plunged into utter darkness. Here, nearly one kilometer beneath the ocean's surface, the light of the sun could never penetrate. Other than the occasional blue flash of luminescence from specially adapted creatures, the black of the Deep was absolute. Johnny's triton form adjusted magically to the massive pressures and near-freezing temperature, but even his highly sensitive eyes were of no use in the trench.

His tonal, however, had no trouble navigating, even as a light flurry of what seemed snow began to drift across the elementals' trail. Johnny experimentally stuck his tongue out and found it to be a gritty, slightly sweet substance. He knew instinctively that he could feed off it in an emergency, but he tried not to think too hard about where it came from or what it was made up of.

With no one to speak to and nothing to look at, Johnny began to reflect on his hot-headedness. When he and Carol had escaped Mictlan with their mother six months ago, he had dreamed of using his shapeshifting in the real world to balance the injustice he saw day in and day out. Then he had jokingly told his parents about his idea to become the Hispanic Captain America—Capitán de las Américas, he had quipped—and, well, they hadn't been too receptive.

"Sorry, *m'ijo*," his dad had said. "These powers are just too dangerous and too important for you to use that way. Plus, think about all the media and government scrutiny that would fall on the Valley."

His mom had made him store Huitzilopochtli's robe. "*Olvídalo*. What if Tezcatlipoca's servants can sense you using it? Too risky."

There had also been a stern lecture from Pingo late one night when he had snuck out to track down a particularly nasty trafficker who had recruited kids from Veterans as drug mules. "Twin naguales," he had whispered after escorting Johnny back to his house, "are too valuable to the cause of Order to engage in petty human misdeeds. Can't keep exposing yourself, partner!"

So for six months, his need to right wrongs had been building and building, the pressure becoming harder and harder to contain. His little prank on Cody Smith, that idiotic bully, had helped some, but his guts still roiled with outrage.

Now here was this really nice mermaid—intelligent, kind, brave, beautiful—getting caught up in the middle of a crazy clash between chaos and order, kidnapped by aquatic angels probably just to mess with Johnny and Carol, to separate them, to push them a little further toward Tezcatlipoca's plans. Johnny wasn't stupid. He knew it was a trap. But sometimes you have to spring a trap. Sometimes waiting for the inevitable just makes things worse. Your only chance is to face the danger head on.

Like the Martinez kids—those mean neighbors that had terrorized the twins' childhood. Johnny could still remember when little Raquel Martínez had invited Carol over to play Barbies—the catch had been that Carol had to bring her own, which were a lot nicer than the cheap *pulga* knock-offs that Raquel had.

Johnny had known it was a trick, but Carol was so excited to go on a play date that he had just kept his mouth shut. When she'd come back empty-handed, crying, he had balled his six-year-old hands into fists and asked what was wrong.

"The dog ate my Barbies!"

"Did you see the dog do it?" he had asked.

"No. Raquel did. She spanked the dog, but my Barbies are gone!"

"No, they're not."

His mother had taught Johnny to stand up for himself, to get the right change back at the store, to exchange the toy from his kid's meal if he got a duplicate at a fast food joint. He wasn't going to let Raquel Martínez steal his sister's dolls.

So he had marched across the street, opened the door without permission, walked right into Raquel's room and caught her playing with the stolen Barbies. Without a word, he had snatched them from her hands. Then he had looked over at the cheap imitations discarded in a corner.

"Those yours?" he had asked.

The rage on her face had been all the answer he needed. He crossed the room and smashed his foot against the dolls again and again.

Man, had he gotten in trouble! His parents had put him in time-out, taken away his Nintendo and TV privileges. But it had been worth it. Not just the look on Carol's face when he gave her back her Barbies.

The defeat in Raquel's eyes.

It was ugly. He knew it was the part of him that Tezcatlipoca was counting on. The bit of chaos amid his love for order and creation.

But he needed it now. He needed that pure, righteous indignation.

It wasn't long until Johnny realized that the flashing green, blue and yellow lights ahead weren't deep sea creatures, but distant water elementals. Pinching a twisted tooth between his forefinger and thumb, he shifted into a six-meter-long sleeper shark with a gruesome and powerful jaw. He began to coast in a leisurely pattern as if quietly hunting for prey, all the while moving closer to the ethereal glow.

Eventually he drew near enough to make out a ledge that jutted out from the trench wall forty meters below its lip. There he saw Ana, bound to an outcropping of rock by a mesh of blue-green energy. Her eyes were closed, and her head floated loosely.

When he got a good look at the tlaloqueh who had taken her, Johnny understood why she had passed out. These elementals were twice the size of Xomalloh, and their bodies flickered with coruscating skeins of electricity, as if lightning danced impatiently inside them. There were three—one the same emerald green as the exile, another with an aquamarine crystal in its chest, and a third who glowed the bright yellow of marigolds. This last elemental was clearly the leader. Larger than the other two, it wielded huge weapons and groaned incomprehensible orders in a voice with the power of a flood.

Johnny turned away as casually as he could and spiraled up the trench wall till he was out of sight over the lip. Then he transformed into a dozen spider crabs, balancing his consciousness across the group as he walked his multiple long-legged bodies to where the ledge was and began crawling them down the wall and toward the princess.

Randomly snatching at passing krill the way a cast of normal crustaceans would, he turned his attention to the rock that Ana was bound to. Inside, he could sense microorganisms, hardy colonies of miniature plants that responded eagerly to his Green Magic.

Grow, he muttered to them, feeding them with xoxal. *Multiply. Here's all the energy you could want. There's more if you'll just keep expanding...*

There came the quietest of cracks. His plan was working. Soon the rock would burst, freeing Ana. And then—

Without warning, a water elemental streamed down at him from above, blasting at his crab colony with a wave of energy. His bodies skittered away in multiple directions.

"One of the *nahuatlin*, brothers!" the newcomer cried, and Johnny realized that this was Xomalloh.

What a freaking jerk! He betrayed us!

Johnny came together and shifted into an octopus, reaching out to grip the rock and crack it further, but the elementals converged on him, slashing with their magical aquatic blades and blasting bolts of power at him. He became a long cusk eel and slipped his way around the blows, directing more and more savage magic at the rock in hopes of making it shatter.

The largest of the tlaloqueh seized Johnny in a massive hand and slammed him against the ledge, stunning him. Johnny didn't quite pass out, though. He was aware of being bound to the rock alongside Ana. He couldn't move. Couldn't reach the Little People's bracelet, tight around his fishy gut.

I can't face these freaks like this. I need to be able to talk. I need hands.

He was desperate. His tonal struggled with him, wanting to free the jaguar, wanting to attack.

No way! We'd be crushed in a second. It has to be a deep sea creature, okay? Come on, dude. Why do you need the DNA again, huh? It doesn't even make any sense. You know the shape. You've shifted into it before. JUST REMEMBER, for the love of God!

A surge of power came from deep within himself. Surprise. Eagerness. A sense of surety. A promise that all would be fine.

Johnny, risking everything, decided to trust his animal soul.

Letting go, he became a triton once again.

"Hey, there," he called to his captors. "I see you're hanging with the Fatherless now. What a perfect name for the back-stabbing punk, huh?"

The lead elemental turned to stare at him, its bright anise eyes shimmering with rage. "Silence, human. You are among your betters."

"Whoa-ho-ho! My betters? You guys? Yeah, right. Bunch of minor lackeys of a minor god."

Ana had awakened and now turned to face him in horror. "Johnny, I do not believe you should antagonize them thus!"

"Ah, whatever, princess. They're just bullies. I've faced up to enough of them."

Xomalloh moved close, dwarfed by his companions but still imposing. "You are addressing Iyauhquemeh, mage, one of Father Tlaloc's four generals. Show him due respect or suffer the consequences."

"Ee...yow...kay...may? Gah, that's a mouthful, man. Can I just call you 'Yowzers'? That's a pretty tight nickname, if you ask me."

Iyauhquemeh brought his translucent face just centimeters from Johnny's. The goggle eyes glinted maliciously as it bared its long, sharp teeth. "My father is no minor god, little beast. He ruled the Earth during the Third Age and then let it shrivel in fiery drought when its inhabitants failed to please him. Rain and sea, thunder and lightning all bend to his command. And my siblings and I work his will upon the world even now, at the waning of the Fifth Sun."

"Blah, blah, blah, you're millions of years old and have seen it all, uh-huh. I know. I heard the same whiny tale from the dudes in Mictlan. Do you guys have like a support group for boring ancient deities or something? Do you share talking points? Because, yeah, I'm falling asleep here, Yowzers."

"Call me not by that name, mewling knave!"

"See, now I *know* y'all consult with each other. That's like your favorite insult. But, okay. Let me think of other things to call you and the rest of the Green Lantern Corps...How about Sinestro? Cyborg Superman? Arkillo? What's wrong, guys, not keeping up with the DC universe?"

"Silence, Juan Ángel Garza," the elemental snarled, "or I will reduce you to a stream of blood adrift in the Deep."

Ana made a frightened sound, but Johnny smiled as broadly as he could.

"That's what I figured. You already know my name. That means Tezcatlipoca is orchestrating this with your pops. And *that*," here he gave a little laugh, "means you can't kill me, no matter how much you want to."

Iyauhquemeh floated back a bit, the gold shimmer within it flickering wildly. Then it, too, spread its mouth wide in a horrifying smile.

"That much is true, nagual. I cannot kill you. Yet nothing prevents me from ripping the life from the siren that you so desperately wish to free."

And as he lifted his blade of water and light, Ana began to scream.

CHAPTER TWELVE

"No, no, no..."

Carol rushed over to the boulder where her brother had just been resting. There was no sign of him anywhere.

Johnny? Johnny, where are you?

He didn't respond. She couldn't feel him. Her heart began to pound; her stomach ached with apprehension. Shrugging off her exhaustion and pain, she swam back to the others.

"Johnny's gone!"

Enehnel muttered a curse. Mihuah rubbed her temples. Tenamic gripped his staff tighter.

But the castellan simply shook her head. "Then he is a fool. We still cannot pursue. We are in no condition to face off against Lords of Water, Lady Carol. They would destroy us."

Carol was about to insist, angrily, when Tenamic said, "It would be more foolish not to pursue. If the boy reaches them, who knows what he may be compelled to do? We cannot risk the possibility that savage magic will fall into the hands of Chaos. Carol, you and I must attempt to head your brother off, to dissuade him from this course of action."

The castellan remained silent, so Carol turned to Captain Xicol. "And you? Isn't your job protecting the Royal Family? Aren't you going to do something? At least for the princess?"

His grey-striped face stolid and serious, Xicol gritted a reply. "Of course. I told Johnny I would accompany him. I do not comprehend why he left alone."

Castellan Nalquiza put her hand on the pommel of her sword. "No. I forbid it."

"Then make me face a court-martial upon our return. I will not sit idle while the princess is harmed." Turning to the dozen guards who had not been injured, Xicol lifted his hand. "I need four tritons. Who volunteers?"

Enehnel and three other young guards came forward.

"The boy's a true nuisance," Enehnel said, "but I'll not see him rush into danger without support."

Tenamic gestured with his staff. "Very well. We must be off immediately. I will employ magic, drawing on ihiyotl to alter the water around us, creating a warmer, faster-moving current so that we will perhaps outpace our rogue nagual."

With the glow of his staff cocooning them against the dark, the seven of them dove into the trench. Tenamic muttered obscure incantations, and the water around them began to stream past, shedding its cold and propelling them forward.

Carol's palms ached as she worried about her brother. It was a familiar feeling, one she had experienced again and again when they were kids.

Once, when they were in third grade at Adame Elementary School, a couple of retained fifth-graders had started picking on younger kids, calling them names, tripping them, the typical behavior of mistreated children who learn from their parents to take their frustrations and self-hatred out on others.

Though the twins, rather tall for their age, hadn't become the targets of the bullies, Johnny had finally got tired of waiting for the adults to do something about the problem. He had confronted the boys in the bathroom and threatened to take care of them himself if they didn't back off.

They hadn't said anything. They just looked at him sullenly, their silence a greater menace than Johnny could realize.

That Saturday, when the twins were out in the neighborhood, tooling around on their bikes, the boys had yanked Johnny to the ground and started kicking him. Carol, frantic, had rushed back to the house, grabbed her brother's BB rifle, and returned to threaten them. They stopped the abuse long enough for Johnny to get his wits about him and punch them both in a strategic spot that sent them sprawling.

Carol had covered for her brother at home, inventing a story about how they'd used plywood at a nearby construction site to make ramps and try to jump cinder blocks.

"Johnny's kind of clumsy," she had said. "He fell and smashed his face up."

A little dubious, their parents had bought the lie. For a time, the twins had been left alone by the bullies, but there was always something. Johnny was always finding new injustices to fight.

Why does he keep biting off more than he chew? I always end up rescuing him.

For the best part of an hour, the team slipped past blurs of bioluminescence, until one set of lights ahead kept growing in size.

"Elementals," Enehnel said. "Four of them."

"Yes," agreed the Archmage. "One is Xomalloh. He must have betrayed our presence in hopes of regaining his place among the Lords of Water."

Carol could see them now. Johnny and Ana were bound to a rocky knob. The largest of the elementals, lit by a golden interior light, leaned close to her brother, making threatening gestures. She could see the wicked smile on the boy's face. She knew what was coming.

"Oh, God. Do something, guys. Johnny's going to screw this up."

Xicol barked orders at his men. They shot out in four different directions, unslinging their spear guns and taking aim.

The golden elemental raised a wicked-looking blade of light and water. Ana's scream trembled frantically through the water.

The guards fired at the Lords of Water. As the spears passed harmlessly through their insubstantial forms, the elementals spun as one. Ana was forgotten momentarily as they began to hurl discharges of power at the guards, who barely managed to twist out of the way.

With shaking hands, Carol seized her necklace, looking for an option, anything, that could keep her brother and the merfolk alive.

Her fingers stopped at a bit of baleen.

Bad idea. Insane. Too deep. Too risky

But there was no other choice.

"Tenamic!" she shouted. Bolts of energy sliced the water around them. At any second, they would be dead. "I need you to change the water around me. A huge bubble, a lot less salty and dense."

"What? Are you mad? I have never attempted—"

"I don't care! Do it now. A six-rod sphere of pressurized water, or I'm dead and so is everyone else!"

The Archmage pulled his staff tight against his chest, closed his eyes, and began to shudder with the effort of the sorcery.

Carol uttered a silent prayer.

Tonantzin, Quetzalcoatl, Matlalcueyeh, Huixtocihuatl—my life is in your hands. Give Tenamic the strength he needs. And, oh, mighty gods, HEAR MY SONG!

With fierceness born of boundless love, Carol seized the baleen in her fingers and bid her tonal to transform. There came an agonized groan as her massive new form displaced thousands of liters of seawater. Around her, scintillating like the promise of sunlight, Tenamic wove a vast pressurized bubble, fifteen meters in diameter, that kept the crushing Deep away.

At the speed of thought, her tonal drew from the vast knowledge of the humpback whale, wise beyond her comprehension, at humbling unity with sea and earth and sky. She knew at once its ancient and glacial language, the songs of a thousand generations, aching hymns whose subtle meaning surpassed the greatest verse ever composed by human hand.

And in that tongue, with those leviathan lungs, with that behemoth voice, she began to sing a sweet and playful tune from her childhood, one that echoed with community and joy, focusing the warbling low frequencies at the Lords of Water:

A la víbora, víbora,
De la mar, de la mar,
Por aquí pueden pasar.
Los de adelante corren mucho,
Y los de atrás se quedarán,
Tras, tras, tras, tras.

Una mexicana que fruta vendía,
Ciruela, chabacano, melón o sandía.
Verbena, verbena, jardín de matatena.
Verbena, verbena, la virgen de la cueva.
Campanita de oro déjame pasar,
Con todos mis hijos menos el de atrás,
Tras, tras, tras tras.
Será melón, será sandía,
Será la vieja del otro día,
Día, día, día, día.

El puente está quebrado,
Que lo manden componer,
Con cáscaras de huevo,
Y pedazos de oropel,
Pel, pel, pel, pel.

The waves of sound thrummed with unmeasured violence, smashing into the elementals: *PEL! PEL! PEL! PEL!* Their watery bodies were blasted away; their heart-gems cracked, flung into the Deep; their haughty glow faded into darkness.

As the bonds trapping Johnny and Ana crackled and then disappeared, Carol shifted back into siren form. Tenamic slumped, drained and feeble. She swam to him and held him in her arms.

"Thank you," she muttered in his ear. "That was incredible. Come, just a little light now. Let's guide everyone back."

Captain Xicol took the Archmage's arm. "Let me bear this

burden, Lady Carol. You…you have performed a wonder I would have sworn impossible. To defeat four Lords of Water! Years from now bards will sing of this victory. A savage mage, wielding sacred songs, felled one of Tlaloc's generals. Amazing."

Johnny rushed up and gave Carol a spinning hug.

"¡No manches, güey! You just went all Aquaman on those elementals! Holy crap that was awesome!"

"Someone had to save your butt. As usual, I drew the short straw."

"No, pos, thanks, Sis."

Ana, shaken but physically fine, embraced her as well. "That was well done, friend. Iyauhquemeh is one of the four Eldest, firstborn sons of Tlaloc and Xochiquetzal. This deed of yours will be recorded in our annals, to be shared in Retellings for generations to come."

Johnny smiled. "Songs and history books, huh? I just want to mention for the record that I turned into a bunch of crabs. I'm hoping that merits, you know, a footnote or something."

Ana put her hand on his arm gently. "Setting aside all jests, it was a foolhardy yet very brave thing you did, coming here alone to rescue me. I will not soon forget it."

Carol couldn't help but grin at the smitten look in Johnny's eyes.

Two hours later they rejoined the rest of the expedition, huddling miserably around faintly glowing globes at the edge of the trench. Castellan Nalquiza listened impassively as her guards reported all that had transpired. She withheld comment, instead giving orders.

"Sleep for a half-watch. Then we depart for the waystation."

The guards hammered spikes into the rock and lashed nets in place so that sleepers would not drift off. Carol wrapped herself up in this strange hammock and tried to sleep despite the adrenaline and cetacean memories bubbling within her.

Just as she was slipping into dreams filled with lonesome whale song, she heard Tenamic whisper, "The girl is the more dangerous of the two. We must keep close vigil over her."

Then the ancient hymns transported her, and she heard the waking world no more.

CHAPTER THIRTEEN

Verónica Quintero de Garza rushed in jaguar form from bow to stern, slamming into man-fish and tumbling them from the yacht into the sea, where a dozen pink dolphins beat at the gilled humanoids with powerful tails. Captain Sandoval and his three sons shot harpoons, bullets and flares into the water elementals that surrounded them, but these attacks were in vain.

Iyauhquemeh rose high on a sea swell, golden energy building to a crescendo in its chest. Then it sent a shuddering wave of power crashing against the *Estela de Mar*, and the boat exploded into fragments of wood, hurling the jaguar into the foaming waves, unconscious. Dolphins rushed to rescue her, but it was too late. The monsters surrounded her, seized her and dragged her down into the sea.

The scene faded. Johnny found himself shivering with rage and sorrow upon the strange sands of Mictlan, where he and Carol had begun their search for their mother six months before.

Xolotl, the massive red-furred dog-twin of Quetzalcoatl, looked down at him with large, compassionate eyes.

"No!" Johnny wept. "Tell me that's not real!"

"Ah, Juan Ángel, if you're asking me whether your mother just died, then no. What you have seen is simply a possibility. Rather, a probability. About three days from now, that battle could very likely occur. I tell you because you have to save her, son. Her death would be horrible in many ways. What it would do to your soul is especially worrisome to us."

"But we would have to turn around right now to reach her in time, Xolotl! And what would happen with the Shadow Stone then?"

The great canine muzzled away his tears. "Don't worry, Juan Ángel. Continue with the mission. When the time comes, you will be given a way. Trust me. And when that path is opened for you, take it without hesitation. For what is to come, you will need your family more than any power or skill. Take care of her first, do you understand?"

The bleak landscape of Mictlan began to fade.

"Wait!" he cried. "I've got more questions."

"I know. But you must act of your own volition, son. Remember, though—when all seems lost, tell Carol to remember the well. Tell her to sing."

Then the darkness of the Underworld grew deeper and deeper till it swallowed Johnny completely.

He awoke with a start.

"About time," called Enehnel. "Thought we'd have to drag your unconscious body all the way to Atlan, lazy bones."

The company was breaking camp, stowing their gear on the few remaining pack sharks. Johnny unraveled himself from his net, yanked up the spikes, and handed them off to a nearby guard. "Thanks."

Swimming groggily to his sister's side, he told her about the danger their mother was in and Xolotl's promise of a path.

"Oh, God," she muttered in distress. "I didn't destroy them.

Just made them really mad, huh?"

"It's okay, Carol. We can't be that far now. It's in the hands of the gods to get us to Mom once we've stopped Maxaltic. I trust Xolotl."

"Sure, me too, but this is pretty stressful."

The group was soon heading south and down. The water grew even darker, denser. The magic inherent in all merfolk combated the crushing pressures as they descended another kilometer.

Johnny's vision and the motives of the tlaloqueh were the main topics of conversation as they traveled. Mihuah suggested that they might be working with Maxaltic, trying to block the company from reaching Atlan, but Johnny wasn't so sure.

"I really doubt the prince has got the clout you need to call up the Lords of Water. I mean, sure there's a connection, but the elemental attack is probably more Tezcat's attempt to mess with our heads—mine and Carol's. He's cool with Maxaltic getting the Shadow Stone and all, but we're his real weapon, if he plays us right."

Tenamic agreed somberly. "He wants you out of sorts, so that by helping to stop the end of the world, you are pushed closer to destroying the cosmos."

"That certainly will never happen," Ana countered. "History shows us that time and again the Lord of Chaos underestimates the power of love and creation. Try as he may, I cannot believe that he will bend the twins to his will or trick them into fulfilling his plans."

"Thanks, Princess," Carol said. "With allies like you all, our parents, the Little People, the gods of order, I know we can stand firm."

Johnny gave her a thumbs-up. He had to admit, his sister always found the positive side to things.

After two hours, they were almost at the floor of the Acapulco Trench, and the Archmage drew a brighter radiance from his staff to reveal a horrific edifice rising from the ooze. Jagged towers jutted at different heights like the teeth of a mutant predator, surrounding an irregular dome that reminded Johnny of a beached jelly fish. As they approached, crystal tubes that snaked along the waystation like gnarled veins began to glow faintly, illuminating squirming eels and other monstrous forms carved all over the hewn stone.

"Spells sense our presence," Tenamic explained, waving away the castellan's worries. "Nothing inhabits this place now beyond the dumb creatures of the Deep. It has long been abandoned."

Nonetheless, Nalquiza had her guards spread out and secure the area. The Archmage sought for an entrance to the ancient building, while Johnny and the others stared at a series of strange statues, some carved in bas relief, others seeming to partially escape the facades, while still others stood partially plunged into the thick mulch that coated the floor of the trench. Many were likenesses of tlacamichimeh, the man-fish that presumably had built the waystation; others seemed to represent strange gods or scary, prehistoric beings.

Johnny got tired of looking at the nasty things; even the bizarre architecture, which had initially struck him as jaw-droppingly awesome, became annoying, fast. He ended up staring at sea cucumbers crawling through the ooze below him and sea lilies trying to catch food with their feathery appendages.

They had been waiting more than a half-hour when shimmering lights in the distance brought the guards together, in preparation for a possible confrontation. But as the illumination approached, they were relieved to see a string of merfolk. Royal guards. Their reinforcements.

Castellan Nalquiza swam up to meet them, saluting with special solemnity an armored, orange-spotted siren.

"I knew it," Ana remarked. "Mother has sent Marshal Cenaman. I would have preferred Marshal Mintoc."

"Cenaman is, after all, second in command," Mihuah remarked.

Johnny couldn't resist the obvious joke that only Carol would get. "Yeah, I like mint gum better than cinnamon, too."

Oh, wow. That's possibly the worse pun you have ever uttered, Johnny.

"Ignore him," Carol said when the two sirens looked at him in confusion. "I take it you two know the marshal?"

Ana nodded. "Yes. When we were children, *Lieutenant* Cenaman was the guard in charge of protecting noble children. She had a young daughter then, Zamache, who was allowed to play with us. The lieutenant often chastised us for what she considered bad behavior just as fiercely as she did her own child, attempting to impose a sort of military discipline."

Mihuah laughed. "Oh, but we were entirely too wild and arrogant for her stern commands. I suppose I was the ringleader, being the oldest."

Ana touched her arm conspiratorially. "Do you remember

when you led us on that escapade to the Midnight Gardens?"

"Oh, by the goddess, yes! Had it not been for your brother, we surely would have been discovered."

The princess gave a little sigh. "Yes, he was different then. Though he had reached the age of adulthood, he never treated us as inferiors and he always rescued us from our own foolishness."

"And from the insufferable scolding of Cenaman," Mihuah added.

Johnny noticed that his sister turned away from them, her brow crinkling the way it did when she was trying to figure out something strange.

What's up? he asked her.

Maybe nothing. It's just that, uh, Mihuah gave me the impression that she had very little contact with Maxaltic when she was a kid, even though they were betrothed. Doesn't seem to fit with this little anecdote, though.

Weird. Why would she lie about something like that?

I don't know. It's probably nothing, though. Perhaps she was just trying to distance herself from a traitor?

As the new guards arranged themselves for inspection, Castellan Nalquiza addressed the expanded company. "We are all thankful to the goddess that our scouts have guided our sisters and brothers here to reinforce our ranks as we embark on the next stage of our mission. Marshal Cenaman, my second-in-command, has brought two hundred guards under royal orders approved by the Assembly of Calpolehqueh. Our directive is clear—proceed to Atlan with all haste and stop Prince Maxaltic from recovering or using the Shadow Stone. Archmage Tenamic, have you discovered the entrance to this eldritch edifice?"

"Yes, Castellan. Yet it behooves us to advance with caution, as the former masters of this waystation may not have wished it disturbed."

The Archmage's suspicions were confirmed once a small group of them entered the building. Several of the newly arrived guards led the way, one a little too eagerly. As soon as the entrance irised open, the triton rushed inside, hand on the hilt of his sword. A volley of darts burst from one of the walls, and only Tenamic's quick blast of power kept the guard from being killed.

"Sensitive to changes in water pressure and displacement," he cautioned as they hauled the wide-eyed triton back. "Let us wait a moment to allow equilibrium to establish itself."

After a few minutes, they slowly made their way down the main corridor to a hub with multiple archways ranged in an irregular polyhedron, as if the nexus had been grown haphazardly like a crystal. A glyph glimmered above each.

"Anybody read man-fish?" Johnny quipped.

Ana floated up toward an archway above them. "I believe it is Middle Apantic, though scrawled as if by a child. This reads 'Observation Tower.' "

She glanced about muttering the different names to herself. Johnny wondered how in the world she knew such an ancient language.

Mihuah apparently noticed his befuddled look. "A Royal Historian must learn all the languages in which our annals have been written. Middle Apantic, if I am not mistaken, was still in use up to about 10,000 years ago among our ancestors."

"Come on, this place can't be *that* old, Mihuah."

"Well, probably not. But the tlacamichimeh are much longer-lived than we are. Only during the last millennium have they begun to learn the newer tongues."

"Here." The princess pointed to an archway at a forty-five-degree angle from the main corridor that was titled 'Map Room.'

This time the guards were a lot less gung-ho about entering the new corridor. When the low hum began, there was time to slip into shallow niches along the wall as a sickly green wave of energy rushed down toward the hub.

Johnny glanced up and down the corridor till he saw the crystal skull encrusted in the stone a little way ahead.

"Tenamic," he called, pointing at it.

"Ah, there it is. Well done, Johnny. It senses the heat and shape of our bodies. The builders of this place despised the Atlacah and sought to keep us from exploring it too deeply even after they abandoned it."

Closing his eyes, the Archmage muttered a spell and sent a bolt of white fire crashing into the sensor, which cracked and went dark.

"I believe the way is safe now," Tenamic said, leading the group a few more meters into an uncharacteristically perfect sphere. It was filled with smaller crystal spheres of varying sizes, floating haphazardly, onto which maps had been etched.

"Uh, that's a lot of maps," Johnny said. "How do we find the right one?"

Ana grinned. "You are focusing on the little details, friend. Take a look at the wider world."

She stretched out her arms, and Johnny saw it—the walls of the room itself were a huge map, finely detailed, different points sparkling with a form of chemical or magical light. Johnny recognized North America's Pacific coast below him. He dove toward it, and the others followed.

Tenamic tapped the butt of his staff against a red dot. "Is this where we are now, Princess?"

Ana came closer, ran her fingers across the glyphs. "Yes, that represents the waystation."

Everyone looked south from that point, hoping to see an indication that Atlan was close by. The dark line of the trench skirted the Mexican coast, but there was no indication of where the ruins might be.

Her fingertips tapping the glyphs, Ana wondered aloud, "How does one get to Atlan from here?"

All around them, a snarling voice gurgled and wheezed.

"What the holy heck was that?" Johnny exclaimed, his eyes scanning the map room.

Tenamic put a hand on his shoulder. "It was the voice of a tlacamichin. Conserved by sorcery in this chamber."

Carol turned to Ana. "And what did it say?"

The princess looked at her fingertips and then at the glyph. "It says 'restate query.' Oh! It did not understand. I know what to do."

She pressed her fingers to the glyphs and grated a question in the ancient language.

A flickering blue line shot out from the red dot representing the waystation, traveling along the trench for the entire length of Mexico and a bit beyond before terminating in another red blotch.

The disembodied voice spoke again. Ana translated.

"Atlan lies 600,000 rods south, off the coast of Kihtyei." She blanched. "That is an ancient name for the land of Cuauhtem-allan."

Guatemala, Carol translated.

Yeah, I know. Map's right there. Besides, I've been speaking Nahuatl for longer than you, Sis.

Oh, I forgot. A whole six months longer. But Guatemala? That's like fifteen hundred kilometers from here, Johnny! What the heck are we going to do?

Tenamic was clearly thinking the same thing. "By the goddess! 600,000 rods? It would take us twenty days to reach Atlan."

Mihuah began swimming along the blue path that had lit up between the waystation and the Abyss.

"Why is it shimmering?" she asked aloud.

Carol dipped toward her, and together they examined the route.

"There is a glyph, hidden in the flickering!" Mihuah exclaimed. "Do you not see it, Ana?"

Without removing her fingers, the princess leaned closer. "Yes! It reads 'half-watch by Roqha.' The name is familiar...ah! I recall it now. Roqha is what our ancestors called the Atoyatl."

One of the guards made a dismissive gesture. "That's foolishness. The Atoyatl is a story for children. A fairy tale."

Johnny looked at him and then back at Ana. "Wait, hold on. Humans in the house. What is this Roqha-Atoyatl thing?"

"A legendary current," Tenamic said, gripping his staff tighter, "that flows as fast as sound, pouring eternally into the Abyss."

"Oh," said Johnny. "I can totally see why he doesn't buy it. That's pretty much impossible."

"Maybe magic?" Carol ventured. "But even then, wouldn't

that kill anyone who tried to travel inside it?"

"Yeah, like being duct-taped to the wing of a jet."

They're not...

...going to understand me. Yeah, I know.

The Archmage seemed to ponder the question for a moment. "Often the patina of legend hides a forgotten truth. While I doubt the existence of a current capable of moving at the speed of sound, it also seems unlikely that the map would lie. If it suggests that there is a way to travel to Atlan in the space of half a watch, I am inclined to investigate. The current must have its source close by, to judge from the illuminated route. I will notify the castellan and marshal about these developments and then take a team to scout ahead. In the meantime, Princess Anamacani, you should lead Mihuah and the twins in an examination of the other maps in this room. Perhaps you will find information that will further aid our mission."

He gestured at one of the guards and began to leave.

"Oh," he added, turning back to glance at them, "take great care in all you do. Be certain to exit exactly as we entered. Who knows what other traps might await intruders in the bowels of this strange place? Or indeed in this very room?"

Oh, great, Johnny muttered sarcastically into his sister's mind. *That's very encouraging.*

CHAPTER FOURTEEN

Thankfully, there weren't any booby traps in the map room. Carol felt pretty useless, wading through the floating crystal globes that represented places she'd never seen labeled with glyphs she couldn't read from a language she didn't know. Ana showed them the symbol for Atlan, a stylized mountain with seven circles, so they concentrated on looking for maps with that mark.

After a couple of excruciatingly boring hours, Mihuah shook her head in exasperation. "I cannot continue, friends. I simply must get out of this chamber. Not only because of how intolerably dull and pointless this exercise is, but also because I must attend to…certain…personal matters."

Johnny snickered. "Oh, that's cool, Mihuah. When you've got to go, you've got to go."

She arched an eyebrow at him and shook her head in mock disappointment.

One of the three guards present drifted to her side. "I'll accompany you, Lady Mihuah."

"No, that is unnecessary. I am going straight out the way we came. Stay here and take my place searching through these inscrutable globes."

With a quick hug of her cousin, Mihuah slipped from the map room.

Lucky her, Johnny complained mentally. *This is really lame.*

Anything that might help us get the mission accomplished faster and help Mom is worth a little annoyance. Besides, I'm pretty sure you don't mind hanging out with your crush, huh?

Again with that? Get a new joke, loser.

Carol laughed despite herself.

Ana looked at them dubiously. "Has anyone ever told you two that it is rude to hold a telepathic conversation in front of others?"

Johnny nodded. "Our mom. Lots of times. Sorry, Ana."

Carol cast about for another sphere to examine. She found one about the size of a Ruby Red grapefruit. Embossed at one of its poles was the glyph for Atlan.

"Hey, guys, look! I found something."

Ana paddled over and took the globe from her hands. "Oh, well done, Carol! This is a map of Sulamala itself, where Epan and Quelel had their final confrontation. I am certain it will help us locate the Shadow Stone before Maxaltic."

"Yay, Carol!" Johnny yawned. "Can we get out of here now? I'm getting hungry and pretty anxious for movement."

"Hopefully Tenamic gets back soon with good news," Carol said, heading toward the entrance. "Johnny's usually too antsy for his own good, but this time I totally agree."

With the other two laughing lightly at her back, Carol led the way back down the corridor to the oddly shaped hub.

There was something waiting for them.

A massive jellyfish.

It filled the entire hub, its gelatinous bell fringed by a thick shock of golden tentacles. Coming from its center and stretching out across several meters were four oral arms—dangerous strands that dangled from the creature's mouth, clutching hungrily.

"By the goddess!" Ana exclaimed. "That is a *minamicqui*, the deadliest jellyfish of the Deep. The venom in those arms can easily kill an atlacatl."

"Crap," Johnny muttered, glancing about. "Is Mihuah okay? Did she make it through before this thing wandered in here?"

"I don't see her," Carol answered. "I think she's safe."

"Or floating in the main corridor after getting stung. Okay, we have to get past. What animal can we use, Sis? Anything armored in your repertoire?"

Carol looked down at her necklace, which floated just above her white yoke. *That's it!* she thought. *We don't have to shapeshift at all.*

"Johnny, we've got the clothing of gods. I'm pretty sure we can make it if we create armored bodysuits with them. Then we can shield these four from getting stung as they move through the hub."

"Not bad, Carol! I like the way you think."

Johnny closed his eyes and soon Huitzilopochtli's cloak had reformed itself into a suit of scalloped black armor covering all but his face. Carol pictured white *oyoroi* of the type that samurai wore in her favorite Manga, and then she coaxed Mayahuel's robe into that shape.

"Alright," she said when she was ready, "let's do this."

The twins dove toward the jellyfish. The oral arms slapped against their armor with sickening thuds, but no poison reached them while they pinned the appendages against the walls.

"Go, quick!" Carol called.

The guards shielded the princess as they swam her quickly through the hub. Once they had crossed, the twins released the jellyfish and joined them in the main tunnel.

There was no sign of Mihuah.

"Thank the goddess," Ana said. "She must be safe."

They finally exited the waystation to find Enehnel and Captain Xicol guarding the entrance.

"Have you seen Mihuah?" Carol asked anxiously.

"Yes, Lady Carol. She emerged not long ago."

"Oh, that's a relief. Captain, there's a huge minamicqui inside. You should probably seal up the entrance and not let anyone else in. We got everything we needed, anyway."

"That seems prudent. Castellan Nalquiza asked to see the three of you once you had finished. Enehnel, please escort them."

As they swam past resting guards, Enehnel looked the twins up and down. "I like this fancy new armor—you'll put even the military pretensions of the castellan to shame, I'm betting."

"Dude, that's your commanding officer you're smarting off about," Johnny said. When Enehnel's eyes went wide and he began sputtering an apology, Johnny cracked a smile. "I'm just joking, man. We all think she's pretty uptight, too."

Enehnel relaxed and gave a bemused laugh.

"Ah. I'd forgotten about your weak jests, boy. Well done."

Carol soon found her samurai armor to not be particularly streamlined or suitable for swimming.

I'm going to go back to the regular siren clothes, she told her brother. *More comfortable.*

I think I'll keep this look for a while, Sis. Just in case.

They found the castellan and the marshal consulting with their staff around weighted maps that lay across a flat boulder. Mihuah was with them, and as the twins approached with Ana and Enehnel, she looked up, a second of confusion crossing her face before she smiled.

"Did you find something after all?" she called.

Ana held up the globe. "Yes. A map of Sulamala. We also found a minamicqui waiting for us in the hub. Had it not been for Johnny and Carol, I doubt we would have made it out alive."

"What? Are you unhurt?"

Ana rubbed her cousin's shoulder. "I am well, Mihuah. The twins have considerable powers to protect."

The castellan clenched her hands into fists. "This time you are unscathed, Princess. We can no longer continue to risk your royal person. Marshal Cenaman carries orders from your mother the Queen. You are to be sent back with a contingent of guards. You cannot accompany us on the final stage of this mission."

Ana turned her head sharply, electric blue dreadlocks whipping about like eels. "Absolutely not. Consider for a moment. Would it not be just as dangerous for me to return to Tapachco, even with an armed retinue, given all the dark forces running amok in the Deep? Besides, I am the Royal Historian, well versed in our ancestral languages. Who else can read the ancient inscriptions that we may encounter in Atlan?"

Nalquiza gestured off toward the distance. "Archmage Tenamic, who even now searches for a current capable of carrying us quickly south, has some knowledge, does he not? Are not the obscure grimoires of his sorcery written in those forgotten tongues?"

"Such is true, Castellan. The lexicon of those magic books is quite different from the words used in public life. You *need* me."

"I must reluctantly agree with Anamacani," Marshal Cenaman said abruptly, pulling her orange eyes away from Johnny's armor, which she had been staring at in envy. "You have encountered great ill in the Deep. She is safest with this entire regiment around her, accompanied by the naguales and the Archmage. And her knowledge of history and language cannot be discounted."

Before the castellan could object or silence her second-in-command, an explosion rocked the waystation, sending bubbling currents of force rolling out in all directions. They were far enough away from the blast that no one was hurt, but they felt warm water push insistently at them as an orange radiance lit the landscape, outshining the regiment's glow spheres. In slow motion, the tallest of the spires collapsed onto the rest of the waystation, causing the strange seething heat to intensify.

In a matter of moments, half of the ancient structure had been obliterated.

"Enehnel!" shouted the castellan. "Go, quickly, and bring me word of any casualties!"

Carol wanted desperately to go with him, but Ana held her and Johnny back. "Wait, friends. This may be a trick meant to lure us close. Let us wait a moment for a report."

The twins reluctantly agreed. Johnny swam in circles, his eyes fixed on the fading ruddy heat of the explosion.

Fire. Underwater. What the heck?

There's probably lots of magnesium or some other really reactive mineral in there. Remember the lab we did last year with Ms. Banda?

Yeah. Damn. If we had still been inside there, Carol…

I know. If we had retreated when we saw that jellyfish, we'd be dead.

More swiftly than they had expected, Enehnel returned.

"No one was killed," he announced. "But a dozen men were wounded, two severely, and we lost most of our sixgills and supplies. The center of the explosion was just outside the waystation, where we had corralled the beasts."

Cenaman slapped a fist into her open palm. "Tenamic warned us you had discovered ingenious traps within the waystation. Perhaps one of the sharks triggered something similar outside the building."

"I'm not sure," Carol cautioned. "A killer jellyfish? An explosion that manages to wipe out most of our supplies? Seems a little too convenient if it's all an accident."

Nalquiza's scar seeped red fury into the rest of her face. "Are you suggesting sabotage?"

"Maybe. Or maybe the prince has agents nearby. Or maybe the Lords of Water are getting their revenge in some twisted way. But an accident? I'm voting no."

But if it's sabotage, who? Could be any of these guys.

Yeah. Ruling out Ana, of course. I don't know, but we need to be on the alert. If there's a traitor here, we don't know them well enough to suspect anything.

O sea, estamos fritos.

Something like that, yeah.

As field medics brought the wounded closer to better attend their wounds, Carol felt a familiar nagging at her mind. It happened to her on tests sometimes. Because of the tension, she was missing something obvious. The answer was right in front of her, but she couldn't see it.

It'll come to me eventually, she thought. *I just hope it comes in time.*

CHAPTER FIFTEEN

Johnny couldn't help but look at everyone with some suspicion. He really hoped the explosion had been a booby trap or enemy attack, but he couldn't shake the idea that there might be a traitor in their midst. He knew just how crappy human beings could be to each other, and he figured merfolk weren't much different. All it took was for some overly gung-ho supporter of Prince Maxaltic to decide he was going to give his hero a fighting chance. Somebody who agreed that humanity's time was up, who wanted to see civilization totally underwater. That fanatical urge to remake the world was already making nut jobs blow stuff up. It wasn't hard to imagine tritons as terrorists, too.

As these grim thoughts kept him occupied, Johnny noticed a group of guards returning from the south under the white luminescent glow of Tenamic's scepter. The command staff gathered to meet the Archmage, and Johnny joined his sister, Ana and Mihuah at their side.

Tenamic reached them and gestured at the glowing ruins of the waystation. "What has happened?"

"An explosion," the castellan explained. "Origin uncertain. It killed most of our pack sharks and wounded twelve of my guards. This tragedy came on the heels of an apparent attempt on the life of Princess Anamacani within the structure—a minamicqui, conveniently awaiting her exit from the map room."

"Then the haste that I would urge is made even more necessary."

"Why? Did you discover the legendary current?"

Tenamic twisted his fingers round his goatee. "Indeed I did. Atoyatl emerges from a massive vent 300 rods south of here. Beside it sits a strange dock, with large crystal pods berthed in three bays. A fourth bay is empty, though it is difficult to determine how long it has been in that state, as the motion of the water allows no build-up of detritus. I estimate each pod can hold fifty individuals with minimal equipment."

Marshal Cenaman glanced behind her at the guards, who were busy aiding the wounded and retrieving what supplies they could. "If we sent back the wounded with an escort, the remaining force could make the journey in the three transports."

"But is the current sufficiently swift?" Castellan Nalquiza asked.

"At Atoyatl's present speed, I fear the journey would take a day and a half. However, I have discovered that the current is capable of much greater velocity with magic."

Johnny pumped a fist. "Yes! Well, you've got that covered, right?"

"The difficulty, Johnny, lies in the *sort* of sorcery required—*eztemalli*, the blood magic of the tlacamichimeh. Therefore are we fortunate to have a pair of twin shapeshifters among us."

Carol tapped her necklace. "There's a problem, then. We don't have any man-fish DNA."

Arching an eyebrow, Tenamic glanced at her with a twinkle in his dead-white iris. "So I had imagined. The Little People were in this instance short-sighted. Yet I believe I have a solution."

He gestured at a guard, who placed a white object in the sorcerer's hands. Tenamic turned and lifted it—a strange humanoid skull with bizarre ridges and jagged teeth. The cranium of a tlacamichin.

"Will this suffice?"

"You'd think so, yeah. But," Johnny said, as he accepted it from the Archmage, "we're not supposed to use DNA from the same organism, according to the Little People."

"Ah, understood. That restriction presents no problem, fortunately, as we discovered a startling expanse of bones not far from the dock. It was clearly the site of some awful internal conflict. We found no atlacah skeletons at all."

Gesturing at her aides to stow the maps, Castellan Nalquiza made a decisive announcement. "Our course is clear. Marshal, select a group to accompany the wounded back to Tapachco and to inform the Queen and King of our progress. The rest of us—including Princess Anamacani—will head to the dock and use these ancient transports to reach Atlan and confront Maxaltic. We leave in ten."

Johnny knew that she meant hundred-beats, which were a little longer than a minute. He decided to spend that quarter hour examining the skull of the man-fish, which looked like it had been bashed pretty hard from behind, judging from the weird dent in the skull.

He was still trying to imagine his brain inside this bizarre cranium when his sister's voice echoed throughout his thoughts.

Johnny! Look up! We're under attack!

A school of thirty massive predators was looming into the

artificial light. They looked a lot like sleeper sharks, only ten meters long and with large, roving eyes that sparkled with malicious intelligence.

"Wayxocob!" Captain Xicol shouted from nearby. "Weapons free! Fire and attack at will!"

As the guards rushed into action, Johnny spun to find Ana. He caught her eye and called out, "What are these things? I need to know what we're up against!"

"Sentient sharks!" she called back. "They have long been servants of the tlacamichimeh!"

Almost as if they'd heard her, a trio of wayxocob broke off and began spiraling toward the princess. Johnny urged his tonal to absorb the shape of the man-fish and transform. He rocketed off toward Ana, yanking the knowledge of how to control the leviathans from the depths of his new form.

STOP! he commanded, using a form of speech that blended telepathy with sonar.

The lead *wayxoc* pulled aside, confused. The others reluctantly followed as they adjusted their course toward Johnny.

Why? Command is attack siren. Kill her.

New command. Siren off-limits. Atlacah mission permitted.

The beasts slowed as they approached him. Johnny felt terror in his gut, but he continued trying to fake them out.

Unusual. Identity. Now.

I am—Johnny dredged up the name—*Sawin Maam. Break off attack. Retreat. Await new command.*

The lead wayxoc bared its gruesome teeth.

No Sawin Maam among the Centlanicah. Well known, the Dwellers of the Deep.

Johnny glanced beyond them. A group of guards had surrounded Ana and were guiding her away as others hurled lances, shot harpoons and used blades in close quarters with the remaining wayxocob.

Another trio of sentient sharks broke off and headed toward Tenamic.

Carol!

I see them. Don't worry. I've got an idea.

Johnny had no chance to watch her actions or lend a hand. The wayxocob began to circle around him, moving in closer.

What lineage? What shoal? What driver?

He knew he could probably find the answers to those weird questions if he tried, but it was pretty obvious that Sawin Maam had been dead too long to matter anymore.

Instead, Johnny scanned the man-fish's fractured memories for information on blood magic. What he found surprised him. Frightened him a little.

Whoa. That's pretty sick. I kind of have no choice, anyway.

Wincing at the pain and the strange coppery taste, he bit into the palm of his right hand. With only a glance at the jagged bite, he dove and quickly swam under the wayxocob, smearing his blue-green blood along their white bellies.

As they twisted and snapped at him, he clenched his webbed fingers into a fist. Xoxal honed his senses, let him see his blood penetrate their cold flesh, seep into their muscles.

He jerked his fist in the direction of the waystation, still writhing hotly in whatever chemical reaction the explosion had set off.

The sharks' bodies went rigid.

Come, he growled at them. *New destination.*

With several punch-like movements of his bloody fist, he send them rushing mindlessly toward the ruins.

Satisfied that they were no longer a problem, Johnny searched for his sister. She had become a school of stargazers, he discovered, butt-ugly fish cursed with eyes on the tops of their heads and gifted with both poison and electric shock. She was harrying the sharks away from Tenamic, stinging them over and over, attacking other wayxocob that came close.

The Archmage wasn't defenseless, of course. He blasted at the enemy with white energy from his staff and intoned quick snatches of sacred song, stunning wayxocob or spinning them unconscious into the Deep.

Between the three of them and the nearly two hundred guards, they managed to win the battle in fifteen minutes, driving off or destroying their attackers.

In the aftermath, the number of wounded had doubled. Johnny was horrified to learn that Enehnel had gotten a huge chunk of his tail bitten away. Shifting back into triton form, he swam to his new friend's side, gripping his hand through the netting that would allow him to be dragged back to Tapachco with the other injured guards.

"Oh, man, I'm so sorry."

"Don't be, boy. Veterans are pampered in our kingdom. And besides, I was getting a little tired of your embarrassing attempts at humor."

Biting his lip, Johnny kept his emotions in check. "Sure. You're just trying to avoid another brutal game of patolli. Getting beaten over and over by a teenager messes with your reputation, huh?"

The young guard gave a weak smile. "Any time you want to look me up in the Hall of Heroes, I'll be ready for a rematch, nagual."

"Okay, then. After we save the world, I'll take you up on your offer."

Letting that be his final goodbye, Johnny joined up with the command staff. Castellan Nalquiza was giving final orders before they set off.

"Our mission's importance is made even clearer by this attack. The princess and the Archmage were specifically targeted, and the twins' intelligence about the make-up of Maxaltic's army seems clearly verified. We can only assume that the prince has taken the missing transport from the dock, leaving the wayxocob behind to impede our pursuit. But we will not be deterred. We leave immediately. I want to be in Atlan before the end of another watch. Then we will confront the traitor and wrest the Shadow Stone away from him if he has already retrieved it."

Thirty minutes later, the army—minus the wounded and their escort—reached another bizarre man-fish structure, one that looked like an outbreak of boils or pimples on the ocean floor. Just beyond it, bubbling hot and fast, the legendary current Atoyatl emerged from a huge crevice, faintly illuminated by deep magma. Partly ringing the source, like two arms pointing into the flow, was a semicircle of stone hollowed out in the center. Into this gaping groove, three transparent pods sat, the way train cars might rest on a track with two on one side and one on the other. There was a huge empty space in front suggesting that a fourth had once been there.

Carol turned to him. "That's the same sort of crystal the water elementals have in their chests."

Tenamic heard her.

"A form of beryl," he clarified, "a mineral compound uniquely able to store great amounts of spiritual energy, whether pure teotl or ihiyotl."

"Okay," Johnny said. "Weird. So the plan is to get inside those gem ships, somehow activate the current's super speed, and then pilot them to Atlan. But they're thousands of years old, and we don't have a clue about how they work."

Gesturing with his staff, Tenamic pointed out a column that jutted up where the arms of the dock came together. "There stands a control tower of sorts. Though I could not decipher all of the inscriptions, it appears there is a way to set a destination and velocity beforehand, and the pods then pilot themselves. While the castellan sees to the loading of guards into each, you and Princess Anamacani should examine the controls and determine the particulars of the process."

"What about my sister?"

"Lady Mihuah and I will accompany Carol to the site of the battle so that she can select a suitable tlacamichin bone to aid you, as from what I could glean, the blood magic required must come from two individuals."

Johnny gave a thumbs-up, dumbfounding his merfolk companions, and made a bee-line toward the tower with Ana by his side. As they approached, strange encrusted veins like those on the waystation lit up.

"Let me see," muttered the princess, floating in front of several columns of inscriptions. "Ah, here it is. 'For automated transport. Controllers activate palm interface with eztemalli. Select destination glyph.' Then...blood and salt! I cannot read the next glyph. Something 'velocity.' What is this symbol?"

Grinning at her frustration, Johnny touched her arm. "Relax, Princess."

He shifted into tlacamichin form, startling her.

"By the goddess, Johnny! Give fair warning before you do that. You are absolutely horrid-looking!"

"Ha!" he snarled in the man-fish tongue. "You just can't appreciate all this scaly goodness. Let me look at that glyph."

Peering with his obsidian-black eyes, he nodded. "Got it. *Wahr-hal.* 'Mind-speak.' Like what I did with the sharks that tried to kill you. Look: 'Select transport number.' Damn, I hope they're just '1', '2' and '3' or something."

Ana gave him an odd look.

"What?"

"It is hardly fair that you can learn in seconds a language that I spent several years studying, Johnny."

He laughed, a horrible sound coming from his fishy lips. "I'm sure we'll find even deader languages in Atlan that I won't know. Your mad translating and historian skills will be put to the test then, big time."

That made her smile despite herself, and Johnny tried not to think of how pretty she looked, blue rosettes on her cheeks crinkling a little as her eyes glittered with humor. "I suppose you are right, as long as I can keep you from seizing a random bone from the ruins and assuming the shape of an ancient human."

"Yeah, I'd pretty much die instantly if I did that." He gestured at the cold, dark water all around. "Pressure would turn me to jelly."

"Ah, thereby eliminating the competition!"

They were still laughing at this macabre idea when Tenamic, Mihuah and Carol rejoined them.

"Figure it out?" his sister asked, gesturing at the tower with a small bone she had recovered.

Johnny lifted a green, scaly, webbed hand and bent his index finger twice.

These dudes have a hard time speaking merfolk or Nahuatl. But yeah. Need your help, though.

Carol nodded. "Okay, here goes nothing."

She shifted into a tlacamichin—the same scaly humanoid form as Johnny, with large webbed feet and hands, glassy black eyes, fish-like mouth, frilly ridges on the head and body and gaping gills.

This is gross, getting inside the spiritual residue of a dead, thinking being.

Yeah. Lots of bits missing, too. But you should be able to get the language and magic stuff easy enough. It's the personality and so on that's pretty much gone.

"I'm ready," Carol said in that guttural, bubbling language. "Where do we put our palms?"

"On either side of the tower, in the weird glowing polygon."

Carol gestured at Mihuah, pointing at the dirk she wore at her waist. While she used it to slice open her palm with a little squeak of pain, Johnny bit into his again.

This feels kind of like black santería, *Johnny.*

Yeah, I know. But what choice do we have?

They slapped their palms against the cold stone, smearing the activation panels with blue-green blood. The tower hummed to greater life, new inscriptions lighting up all over its surface.

Johnny looked up at the line of glyphs that represented possible destinations. With his free hand, he touched *Atlan*.

Do I do the same? his sister asked.

Yeah, I think so. Knowledge of the procedure had begun bubbling up from within his new form, confirming what he and the princess had worked out. *Yes. We both have to do everything. Now we have to use* wahr-hal *to tell it maximum speed. Then, do you see the grid of numbers? One is dark, but we've got to click '2', '3' and '4'.*

Got it. Ready?

"Ready," he snarled. "Three, two, one..."

Maximum speed, they commanded in unison. Johnny felt his blood trigger whatever ancient mechanisms lay below the dock, a physical as well as spiritual grinding that ended in a hollow click.

Behind them, the current's rumbling flow became a thundering, bone-rattling rush. Ana and Mihuah exclaimed something, but it was drowned out by the Atoyatl. Quickly, the twins punched at the numbers.

"COUNTDOWN TO LAUNCH." A gruesome voice boomed even louder than the gargantuan gush of water. "THIRTY. TWENTY-NINE."

Pushing away from the tower, the twins spun to swim with the other three toward the pods, which were now lit up by an aquamarine luminescence. By gestures, Tenamic instructed Ana and Johnny to enter one, Mihuah and Carol another, while he headed toward the third.

Johnny had barely made it inside, pushing the princess through and sealing the door with a slap of his bloody palm, when their pod was shot like a harpoon into the Atoyatl's impossible flow.

CHAPTER SIXTEEN

The fifty individuals inside Carol's pod, through some inexplicable magic, were not shoved back by the sudden thrust. The water sealed in with them shimmered with blue energy as the transport dove deep into the current. Once they'd reached top velocity, the glow receded to a mere illumination in the transparent walls around them.

As they hurtled down the Acapulco Trench at the speed of an airliner, Carol peered ahead at the pod that contained her brother, the princess of Tapachco, and another forty-eight guards. Reaching out, she called to Johnny.

Hey, can you hear me?

Yup. You guys okay?

Pretty much. Por poco se nos pasa.

Ha! We barely made it inside, too. So I guess now we just enjoy the ride, huh?

Sure. Talk to you later.

Mihuah drifted close. "Was that your brother?"

Carol nodded. "Yes. They're all fine."

Pirouetting slowly, she looked over the guards and their officers. Most were impassively resting, but several had nervous looks on their faces. A few gestured at the dark around them, twittering quietly to each other.

"What's got them so panicked?" Carol asked Mihuah.

"Do remember that our older relatives fill our childhoods with tales of the Abyss and the terrors that await mischievous sirens and tritons there. No matter how mature these guards fancy themselves, the fears of our youth tend to survive well into adulthood. Now that we are descending at this breakneck pace into the realm of monsters, you will forgive them a few moments of unease."

Carol thought about silence and the dark, about the attack she had experienced in Mictlan that summer. "Oh, I totally get it. We're all frightened of something. I'll bet that even an up-and-coming diplomat like you, daughter of the minister of state, gets scared from time to time."

The siren's skin darkened slightly, flushed by some emotion. "I am sure I have no idea what you are implying, Carol."

"Maxaltic. You said that when you were a kid, you saw him like a legendary figure. You pretty much suggested that you didn't spend any time with him. But the stuff you and Ana have shared about growing up kinds of contradicts what you told me during our tour. I'm guessing you didn't want me knowing all the facts. So either you're hiding something, or you're afraid."

The siren's gill clefts opened wider, a sign that she was outraged or embarrassed.

"Listen. You can certainly understand the awkwardness of admitting to a stranger that you have a long-standing friendship with the triton she is hunting down. I like you, Carol, but, yes, you scare me. You are young, but you are powerful. I had no desire to be interrogated or perhaps tortured by you for inform-ation."

"What? Mihuah, I would never do anything like that to you!"

"I know that *now*, of course. But on day one? My mother raised me to be very cautious interacting with foreigners, to reveal only what needs revealing. Besides, you had access to Anamacani and others, and all of them are aware of how close Maxaltic and I were before..."

"Before he broke off your engagement? That part's true, I know, from what others have said."

"Yes. Everything else I told you is the truth. I simply kept our childhood friendship from you to make your investigation less complicated. It is not as though that knowledge could have helped you track him down any more quickly. Do forgive me, Carol. I realize now that I should have been absolutely sincere with you about this matter."

Though she was not completely satisfied, and despite something still nagging at her mind about Mihuah's deception, Carol smiled and shrugged. "It's okay. Heck, my best friends have told me bigger lies, and we still hang out."

They hugged briefly, and both excused themselves to rest. Carol stayed near the front of the pod, taking advantage of the glow from the lead transport to observe the trench. The west wall had become a gradual slope; the east wall was still kilometers distant, a flat black expanse even in the meager light. Startled aquatic life rushed by on all sides, caught in the torrential flow of the current, some torn apart by the force to Carol's chagrin.

Beyond occasional tors, boulders, and bubbling crevices, their surroundings remained much the same as they gradually dipped deeper and deeper.

Lulled to drowsiness by the unchanging vista of the Deep,

Carol felt her eyes slowly close. She did not fight sleep. Surprisingly, no dreams or visions came to her.

S he was jerked awake a few hours later when the pod began angling against the current. It was a bumpy ride as it exposed its starboard side to the pounding flow for the space of several turbulent minutes. It exited Atoyatl just behind the other pod and was followed by the third.

Johnny?

Yeah, still here. We're okay. You?

A little jostled, but fine. I guess this is the Abyss, huh?

Looks pretty much like the rest of the Deep to me.

Keep an eye out for ruins.

Carol pressed her face against the crystal, hoping to make out shapes below.

"It would seem we have nearly arrived," Mihuah said, joining her.

"Yes, but I don't see a dock anywhere, much less a sunken continent, do you?"

Just then the pods began to slow with an audible hum as they descended toward a crescent of orange that sizzled against the black of the Abyss. Making swooping spirals, the vessels slipped their way inside a most unexpected space.

It was a cavern, as Carol had imagined, but one so vast she could not make out its far wall, even in the hellish illumination that lit up the shattered interior. This orange-red glow came from sluggish streams of lava that crisscrossed the landscape as far as the eye could see, pooling into infernal lakes in some places. Carol gasped as she saw crumbled towers and buildings beside the nearest of those molten lagoons.

"It's Atlan," she said to Mihuah, awed by what she saw. "The whole place has been sealed deep in the crust of the earth."

Mihuah nodded thoughtfully. "The legend ends with that event: 'And Tlatecuhtli, Lord of the Earth, opened wide his maw and swallowed the island whole.' I always supposed the line to be metaphorical."

With a change to the frequency of their hum, the pods arced toward a transport station, twin of the one they'd launched from.

A fourth pod was visible, but it hadn't docked correctly. Instead, it lay broken against an outcropping of jagged black rock. Carol couldn't see any bodies inside.

Their three vessels hissed to a stop in the berths without any issues at all. The mass of guards swarmed forth into the warmer, less dense water, responding to orders to clear the immediate area, checking for signs of the enemy. A team went to investigate the crashed transport.

Carol joined her brother and the command staff by the control tower. Princess Anamacani was holding the map of Sulamala in her hand and gesturing at the ruins.

"Do you see it? Half-buried in the rock beside that coral-encrusted stone pier? That is the head of the statue of Huehuehteotl, the Old God, which once towered above the harbor of Sulamala."

"Praise the goddess," the castellan muttered. "Our trek is at an end. All information points to this city as the resting place of the Shadow Stone."

"Yup," Johnny agreed. "And that also means that Prince

Maxaltic and his band of merry monsters are here."

Captain Xicol approached. "Castellan, Marshal, a report: there are no remains near the crashed pod. Whoever traveled within made it out alive."

"Was there any indication of how long ago it came here?" Tenamic asked.

"No, Archmage. As was the case at the first transport station, the eddying currents draw silt away. It may have impacted against those rocks earlier today or weeks ago."

"Or indeed in centuries past."

Casting a sober look in the sorcerer's direction, Castellan Nalquiza made a decision. "Marshal, select a contingent to remain behind and guard the pods. We advance on the city at once."

With a hundred and twenty guards and ten officers arranged in a protective sphere around them, the twins, Tenamic, Ana and Mihuah swam toward the shattered remains of Sulamala. Once beyond the harbor, Carol began to panic. Though the vague outlines of broader streets could still be made out here and there, the rest of the city had been basically razed or was covered by strange, shimmering coral. A school of twisted fish exploded from a time-slagged structure. A cloud of bioluminescent organisms drifted overhead. Johnny lifted his hand to run his fingers through it, stirring sparkling eddies.

Ana called for a halt. She stared at the map, swiveled around, searching for something. Then she chirped in annoyance.

"This globe is useless. Nothing here is recognizable after 80,000 years. I cannot get my bearings."

The castellan rubbed at her scars in dismay. "That is ill news. How are we to find the palace?"

"Don't freak out," Carol said. "If we're having a hard time, so is her brother. It might be better for all of us if this place is too wrecked to find the Shadow Stone, anyway."

Nalquiza and Cenaman exchanged a glance that tied her stomach in knots.

"Unless you guys are planning to recover the freaking thing yourselves, of course. Orders from the Queen?"

Before they could respond, a form rocketed out of the ruins below, heading straight at them. Guards lifted their weapons and prepared to attack.

Carol saw that it was a tlacamichin. Lifting her arms, she called out, "Hold on! Don't kill it! Just catch it or something!"

The marshal backed her up with a shouted order, and several tritons launched weighted nets at the creature.

What are you doing, Sis?

Don't you think it's weird that it's by itself? Just hang on. Let me get some information from it. You're on translation duty.

The tlacamichin was thrashing in the grip of four guards, snarling and hissing. Carol dove toward them, shifting into a member of its race. When it saw her, it stilled its movements.

"What are you doing with these atlacah?" it demanded.

"I'm not actually a tlacamichin, sorry. I've assumed this shape so we can talk."

"Shape? Are you a nagual, then? A human?"

"Yes. My name is Carol. Now tell me, who are you?"

The creature's demeanor softened. Carol realized it was a male.

"I do not truly remember, Carol. I lost my name and my shoal many years ago. But I have known humans, and the human children called me Jabalí."

Holy crap, Carol! Johnny sent excitement and wonder. *It's the man-fish from Mom's story. That's insane!*

"Ah, Jabalí," Carol muttered, moving close, gesturing the guards away from her as they attempted to stop her. "You poor soul. We know a fragment of your sad tale, friend. You were kind to those kids when you had no reason to be, when you were lost and alone."

Overwhelmed by emotions she couldn't quite name, she reached out and folded the tlacamichin in a scaly embrace.

When she released him, his black eyes were full of wonder.

"I have been alone for so many years, Carol. I thank you for the feel of your flesh. Tell me what I can do to help you. What is your purpose in this hated place?"

She hesitated a moment, looking around at all the merfolk for whom Johnny was translating their exchange.

Tell him, Sis. The worst that can happen is he's actually working with Maxaltic.

"Okay. A triton, the prince of Tapachco, is trying to get his hands on the Shadow Stone. We're here to stop him."

A sorrowful grimace twisted Jabalí's already gruesome features. "Ah, that damnable device. If you only knew the tragedy it has brought to my people..."

"Tell me."

His webbed hands clutched nervously at the magma-warmed water. "It was during the last time that the seas were clogged with ice, perhaps 20,000 years ago. The Lord of Chaos reached out to us, tempting us with promises of might, of dominance—all Blessed Creatures under our rule. Hungry for power, hating ourselves as less than the others, we fell, Carol. That was a dark age. For all the expansive buildings we wrought, all the magic we mastered, all the nations we laid low, we were lost as a people, any jot of beauty or goodness effaced by our betrayal of creation itself.

"After millennia, at the urging of the Lord of Chaos, we began to raid Atlan, searching for the Shadow Stone. At last it was found, along with a staff carved from the World Tree."

Johnny translated and there was a burst of excited murmuring all around.

"Where were they kept, Jabalí?"

"I do not know, Carol. Somewhere in this city, guarded constantly, awaiting the pleasure of the Lord of Chaos."

"Strange. Why weren't they ever used?

"Again, I do not know. Please forgive me. My memory is faulty, and furthermore what I tell you was passed down over many, many ages. You see, though my people had embraced chaos, a group of individuals faithful to the cause of creation survived in secret down the ages. Their numbers grew, and once the Shadow Stone was uncovered, they revealed themselves. A civil war erupted. Many thousands died."

Carol realized that the field of bones half-buried in slime beside the transport station were probably the result of this conflict.

"And what happened to the stone and staff then?"

"Those opposed to chaos were nearly eliminated, Carol. It took millennia to recover, for our numbers to swell to the point that we could be effective. We returned here mere centuries ago and found them unguarded, perhaps forgotten."

She reached out and seized his shoulder. "What did you do

with them? Where are they now, Jabalí?"

The tlacamichin reached up and laid his cold hand atop hers. "I cannot remember. Forgive me. Something happened…afterward. Some sort of…clash. My mind, Carol. It was…shattered. For more than a century, I have struggled to remember, to reconstruct the events that led to my memory loss. What I do know is that I awakened in a lagoon on the surface world, not knowing who or where I was. The humans were good to me, especially the children. Later I heard the call of my people and made my way back to the sea. But my shoal was gone. All that are left are the degenerate descendants of those who swore fealty to the Lord of Chaos."

Carol groaned in frustration. As her brother translated the last bit, angry and disappointed conversations bubbled and seethed among the merfolk.

Archmage Tenamic swam up behind her. "This is pointless. He has given us nothing of real utility."

"Just hang on, okay? I'm not done asking him questions."

Jabalí glowered at the sorcerer. "I cannot perceive their dolphin sounds, Carol, but I can read lips, and I know Nahuatl. Tell the old triton that I do know one thing—the staff and stone no longer lie here in Atlan. I have searched these broken cities for decades. They are gone."

Johnny relayed this information, and the angry murmuring became chaos. The castellan and marshal sidled close to Carol, panic in their eyes.

Nalquiza squared herself against Jabalí. "Read the words from my lips, tlacamichin. Have you seen the prince or his army?"

"No, scarred siren general. No one else is here. No sentient being has ventured into this cavern for at least half a year."

Marshal Cenaman butted in after hearing the translation. "What about the pod that is crashed near the transport station?"

"I found it thus when I first arrived, warrior, nearly a century ago."

Shuddering with the implications, Carol shifted into siren form. Her eyes went wide with shock.

"Oh, my God, everyone. It was a trick. The whole thing was just a trick!"

They were six kilometers beneath the sea, three thousand kilometers from their parents and the merfolk of Tapachco.

The only protection for everyone they loved had been removed.

There was nothing to stop Maxaltic or Tezcatlipoca now.

The cold, dark expanse of the Deep seemed to filter into Carol's very soul, gleeful and cruel, drowning and freezing every last hope.

CHAPTER SEVENTEEN

Johnny thought his heart would burst. He clenched his fists in desperation.

Mom's in danger. Damn you, Xolotl—you promised me a path! The stupid Atoyatl can't get us back in time, so where is it, huh? Quetzalcoatl told the Little People we'd be "aided in the hour of our greatest need." This is pretty much that hour, dude!

Then it came to him. There was already one person present who fit the bill of *deus ex machina*, wasn't there?

Roughly shifting into tlacamichin form, Johnny rushed down at Jabalí. Carol looked up at him, despair clouding her eyes.

What are we going to do, Johnny? If he kills them...

No one's killing anybody. Just hush. I've got this.

"You. Jabalí. Got a riddle for you. A god told me that when the moment came, a path would be opened for us down here. What do you think he meant?"

The man-fish looked at him oddly, sucking water into his mouth in small gasping swallows.

"Well, you two are twin *nahualtin*. Perhaps you can use the sacred apiyaztli."

Johnny lifted a hand. "Wait. We know what those are. Water tunnels. Our dad's researching some in a temple in Mexico."

"I am not referring to those physical constructs, brother of

Carol. Instead, I mean the conduits used by the gods to pass from one realm to another in a mere instant."

"Okay, okay. That's pretty cool. Good sign. Oh, name's Johnny, by the way. So you're saying there's a sacred apiyaztli *here*? In Sulamala?"

"Yes. In the Temple of Matlalcueyeh. If you will permit me, I will guide you and your atlacah soldiers to it."

Now it was Johnny's turn to give old gill-man a big hug. "Permit you?" he laughed as he pulled away. "Dude, you may have just saved our parents' lives. I'm going to be in your debt for a long time."

Carol had already translated the exchange when he turned to the castellan, shifting to triton form.

"We need to follow him. This is our only chance at stopping the prince and his crazy allies."

"Agreed."

Nalquiza gave the order, and soon the guards had reconfigured themselves into a wedge formation. Jabalí swam at the apex, guiding the regiment over buildings so corroded they might as well have been natural features of the cavern. From time to time Johnny could make out massive columns and sprawling squares, but for the most part magic, time, and theft had reduced Sulamala to nothing.

Johnny glanced at Ana, who was visibly distraught. On the trip down into the Abyss, she had opened up even more to him, sharing her fears over her brother's choices. She really did love Maxaltic, even though they had grown distant since she had become an Air Sage and the Royal Historian.

"I know there is little I can do once we find him," Ana had

told Johnny. "His fate will be in his own hands and yours. Promise me you will try not to hurt him too badly. He has merely been deceived. There is an essential goodness in him. If we capture him, efforts can be made to reform his heart."

Johnny had sworn to do all he could to end the conflict with as little harm as possible. In all honesty, Maxaltic was a small fry in this struggle. Tezcatlipoca was the scum that needed to be eradicated, not the prince.

Now, in the ruddy light of Atlan, Johnny tried to reassure his friend once more.

"It's going to be okay, Ana. We're going to get out of here and stop them before they hurt your people or mine."

She did her best to smile at him, but her blue lips trembled slightly with worry.

"Thank you, Johnny," she managed to say.

They passed over a broad bed of magma, and just beyond it they found a large mound of stone and coral, crested by pale sea grass.

"We are here," Jabalí announced.

Nalquiza and Cenaman had their captains arrange squads in defensive positions around the ancient temple. Captain Xicol and his team accompanied the command staff and civilians as they followed Jabalí through the broad entrance near the summit. Given what he knew about ancient architecture, Johnny figured the temple sat atop a now hidden ziggurat of some sort.

He was surprised to see that the temple's interior was much better preserved than he would've guessed. Soft light emerged from shimmering mosaics on the floor and walls, which were relatively free of the layer of flora that covered so much of the city. Ornately carved columns supported the heavy stone ceiling of the large antechamber. Doorways on either side indicated other rooms, but Jabalí ignored them, swimming beyond, into the temple proper.

The inner sanctum was enormous, fifty meters broad and deep, with a high vaulted ceiling whose aquatic patterns were obscured by dark shadows above. The space was dominated by a platform upon which stood an enormous statue of Matlalcueyeh, her aquamarine headdress splaying wildly like Anamacani's electric blue dreads. The skirt of the water goddess was hewn from emerald, flowing down the platform to pool into a wide, green mirror.

That's got to be the entrance to the sacred tunnel, Carol suggested. *It's a lot like the chay abah we used to get into Mictlan.*

Or the one Tezcatlipoca uses to travel between his home turf and the Underworld. Yeah, I was thinking the same thing.

Maybe obsidian mirrors are for certain places and emerald for others.

Let's hope so. Not too excited about heading back to the Land of the Dead.

"So," Johnny said, turning to Jabalí and forcing his triton mouth to produce the gargling sounds of the man-fish language, "what do we do now?"

"I am unsure, Johnny."

"Fantastic. I'll guess we'll figure something out."

Shrugging in irritation, he reached out and touched the mirror. A tickle of energy flickered across his fingertips. Closing his eyes, he used savage magic to gently probe the crystal.

"Careful, boy," he heard Xicol gasp.

Peeking at the smooth emerald surface, he saw that the water above it had begun to swirl and bubble. Retreating a bit, Johnny watched this movement grow into a frantic roil.

"Well," Carol told him, "this one doesn't stream smoke, but I'd say it's getting ready for transport."

A blinding flash of verdant light caused them all to turn away, but they felt the water around them shudder as something came through. Johnny jerked his head back and saw three massive tlaloqueh emerge from the mirror's surface. Burning in their translucent chests were hunks of raw emerald. They clutched two-handed blades of water and verdant fire.

One of them thundered an angry query: "WHAT MORTAL IS FOOLISH ENOUGH TO DARE THE GATEWAY TO TLALOCAN? WE ARE THE *APIXQUEH*, GUARDIANS OF THE DIVINE WATERS OF PARADISE. NO LIVING BEING MAY CROSS THIS BOUNDARY!"

Castellan Nalquiza surged out in front of the twins, lifting her hands in supplication.

"Hold, puissant Lords of Water! Our need is great. The fate of our world depends on swift travel away from this place."

"WE CARE NOT FOR THE FATE OF YOUR WORLD, SNIVELING SIREN."

With a movement almost too fast for the eye, he thrust his blade through her chest. Immediately, the guards hurled spears and shot javelins at the elementals, but their attack was in vain. The projectiles passed through them harmlessly.

"Retreat!" called Marshal Cenaman, and Johnny felt Captain Xicol's hands on him, dragging him forcibly away.

"No!" he shouted. "I've got to fight them!"

"How, boy? They almost killed you last time!"

Johnny, fuming, allowed himself to be guided in a rush out of the temple, the Apixqueh fast on his tail. Cenaman was already shouting orders at the squads surrounding the mound, and as the elementals burst forth, they were greeted by a flurry of attacks.

Carol, get Tenamic to help you with the whale song gambit. I'll see if I can distract these bubble butts in the meantime.

Got it.

He looked up at the coral and sea grass, looked *into* them with his tonal, called to them with all the desperation in his heart, twisting his will into theirs using Green Magic.

Grow. No need to wait. Grow as fast as you can. Take this shape. Do you see it? Yeah, you want to curl that way, don't you? Come on. Grow.

The flora and fauna on the crest fairly exploded into movement, forming a tight cage of coral and sea grass around the elementals. Glancing over at his sister, Johnny saw Tenamic lift his staff. Captain Xicol floated below him, weapons at the ready.

Another blinding flash of green light reduced Johnny's living cage to microscopic bits. The tlaloqueh began firing coruscating sheets of energy at the merfolk. Before Carol could transform into a humpback whale, one of these bolts ripped through the water right toward the Archmage, who tried to deflect it with his own white fire. The concussion ripped his staff from his hands and sent him spinning off toward a magma stream. Guards hurried to catch him.

Johnny rushed toward Xicol, who was floating unconscious and seriously wounded. Carol darted over, seizing Tenamic's staff.

Johnny, help me! This thing can amplify magic. We need to channel xoxal into it and blast those damn things before they kill anyone else!

Nodding, he gripped the staff as well, his hands between Carol's.

The ivory was ancient. Johnny could barely sense the beast it had belonged to, a terrifying leviathan that had plied the Deep millions of years ago. The arcane glyphs licked at his palms, hungry for magic.

Within him, his tonal snarled with feral joy. This tool it understood.

Calling to its sibling, the jaguar poured itself with eager abandon into the carefully carved staff. The wolf clawed its way along the petrified bone as well.

In that instant, Johnny and Carol were almost one being. There was no need for words or thought. They lifted the staff and aimed, releasing a torrent of white-hot savage magic.

The outer shell of the elementals boiled away in a fraction of a second, leaving their emerald cores exposed. The twins' beam of power slammed into the crystals with such unremitting force that they cracked. Then, with a guttural howl that rattled Atlan from end to end, they shattered into a million glittering shards.

With a convulsive gasp, Johnny pulled his tonal back, releasing the staff.

Carol was left staring at the empty space where the tlaloqueh had floated seconds ago. Johnny saw her glance down at her hands and shudder.

Oh, my God. What did we just do?

He swallowed. For the moment, he couldn't quite bring himself to reply telepathically.

"We saved them, Carol. The only way we could."

All around them, guards were helping the many wounded as captains shouted commands. Ana and Mihuah swam to the twins, bearing a weakened Tenamic between them.

"Those children of Tlaloc," he managed to say, "have existed since the Third Age of the world. Millions upon millions of years. And you obliterated them in seconds."

Ignoring the nausea he felt, Johnny gave a dismissive smirk. "Yeah, well, them or us, Archmage. I don't know what you want me to say."

Wordlessly, Carol handed the sorcerer his staff. He accepted it with ginger care, running a light finger along the glyphs.

"Princess Anamacani," he said, "have you ever read of a Blessed Creature killing a tlaloqueh?"

"No, Archmage. But our history is limited to this age and mostly to our own kind."

Carol shook her head. "Killing's not the right word."

"No?" Tenamic ran a trembling hand through his beard. "Perhaps not. I have no knowledge of the constitution or fate of elementals, to be frank. Yet your power worries me profoundly. It strikes me that you travel the same path as most other nahualtin of your type."

"Soft, now, Archmage." Ana's tone was gentle, but firm. "There is much left to be done. Let us not worry them further."

Carol bit her lip, a clear sign that she was upset. "Worry us with what?"

The princess said nothing, but her face grew grim.

Johnny swallowed heavily. "You've got to tell us, Ana."

She turned away, staring out toward the temple as she spoke.

"Very well. In the eighty centuries since Atlan fell, there have only been five sets of cocoah, of shapeshifting fraternal twins. Of those, three…"

Her voice hitched and she shook her head.

Tenamic spoke softly. "Johnny and Carol, three were bent to the will of Tezcatlipoca."

"Not us," Johnny snapped, suddenly angry. "No freaking way. He already threatened us with his little plan for us, and it's not going to happen."

For the first time, Mihuah spoke, her voice nearly inaudible. "How can you be sure, Johnny?"

"I know my own heart. I know Carol's, too. We'll die first."

The sorcerer looked at them serenely for a moment before nodding.

"And what happened to the…the bad twins?" Carol managed to ask. "Obviously they didn't cause the end of the world. We're still in the Fifth Age."

Ana's voice shook as she turned to face them again. "The magic beings of the world, my friends. They joined together to… to stop those twins."

Johnny's limbs went cold with dread. He suddenly understood the Queen's reaction, the distant treatment of Tapachco's elite. For them, he and his sister were unpredictable, possibly deadly forces.

Tenamic had floated free of Mihuah and Ana. Clutching his staff against his chest, he stared at the distant roof of the impossibly vast cavern.

Carol glanced at him, worry plain on her face, and then moved closer to Ana.

"But two sets of twins were fine, weren't they? They managed their powers. Like Johnny said, so can we."

"I believe you can as well, Carol. That is why I was reluctant to reveal any of this history to you. Consider this very important and mysterious fact—all shapeshifting twins share the same spirit animal, based upon the day of their birth. Why then, are you two different? Why are you a wolf and Johnny a jaguar?"

"Clear mockery of the First Divine Twins," Tenamic muttered. "Quetzalcoatl and his canine form, Xolotl; Tezcatlipoca and his jaguar, Tepeyollotl. These two will doubtlessly clash as violently as those gods, and the universe will regret the very hour of their birth."

"That's freaking ridiculous," Johnny spat. "Carol's my best friend. I'd never hurt her. That can't be why we have different animal souls!"

Ana nodded. "I agree. Though you should both be jaguars, Carol has been gifted with a wolf tonal for a reason we cannot perceive. As for me, I trust in the wisdom of the gods. In the meanwhile, do not lose heart. You have friends who will struggle at your side and draw you back from any darkness."

Tenamic's voice was almost a sob. "I am afraid we cannot afford the risk."

With unexpected speed, he spun and blasted at the twins with energy from his staff. Carol shifted into a school of viperfish, scattering in a dozen directions to avoid the attack. Johnny, who had earlier run his hands through a stream of bioluminescent plankton to collect a sample, now transformed himself into a cloud of the blue fire plants. He opened gaps in his amorphous form to let the bolts pass harmlessly through as he drew closer and closer to the sorcerer, squeezing his form around the staff and wrenching it from Tenamic's grasp.

"Jabalí!" he called as he shifted back. "Grab this old triton for me!"

The tlacamichin was upon them in seconds, wrapping his powerful scaly arms around Tenamic and holding him tight.

Dozens of guards rushed to surround them. Johnny wheeled about, brandishing the staff. The viperfish encircled him like a shield.

There was a moment of supreme tension. Then Marshal Cenaman re-emerged from the temple, bearing the corpse of her commanding officer.

"Enough!" she cried, her voice hitching with sorrow. "What is the meaning of this?"

Ana came to their defense. "The Archmage sought to kill the twins, Marshal. They have subdued him."

"Is this what we are reduced to?" demanded Cenaman. "Our castellan dead, dozens more wounded, and at the first taste of victory, we tear one another apart? Thus will the enemy destroy us without raising a hand."

She let the castellan's body drift into the arms of her aids.

"Now, then. Johnny and Carol, instruct Jabalí to turn Archmage Tenamic over to my guards. We will keep him restrained, I assure you."

Johnny looked at the man-fish. "Let him go, buddy. They've got him."

Guards bound the sorcerer's hands. Tenamic wept openly, but said nothing else. The guards surrounding Johnny withdrew, and Carol resumed siren form.

Cenaman looked at the staff in Johnny's hands and gave a curt salute.

"Shall we attempt this divine passageway once more?"

"Yeah, definitely."

Johnny noticed that the princess was swimming in circles, searching for something.

"What's wrong?" he called.

"Mihuah is missing, Johnny. I cannot find her anywhere."

CHAPTER EIGHTEEN

Still reeling from their losses, from the unexpected betrayal of the Archmage, Carol found her stomach clenching up with dread. Mihuah, missing? Had Tenamic's attacks harmed her? Killed her? Was she hiding somewhere?

"As I pulled Castellan Nalquiza's corpse from the inner sanctum," the marshal said, "I saw Lady Mihuah enter the temple, seeking refuge, no doubt. We will find her inside."

Oh, thank God. I don't think I could handle another freaking tragedy today.

Me neither. Come on. Let's get out of this dump.

She and Johnny were accompanied by Jabalí, Cenaman, Ana and a squad of guards.

Mihuah wasn't in the main chamber.

"She's probably in one of the other rooms we passed," Carol said, heading back. "Pair up. Find her, quick."

Ana, Johnny and Jabalí followed her as she swam through the first doorway on her right. It was a small room with a hole set in the floor.

"Guess there used to be a ladder or stairs," she mused aloud. "Rotted away ages ago. Let's check below."

Diving down the stairwell, she entered a much larger chamber, lit by a strange purple glow.

It came from a large obsidian mirror fixed to one wall.

Floating in front of it was Mihuah. She turned, startled.

There was a young triton in the mirror, head and shoulders above the surface of a lake. The sun shone between tall trees behind him.

"I know that place," Jabalí muttered, raising webbed fingers and gripping his head as if in pain.

"Maxaltic?" Ana gasped.

"Oh, hello there, dear sister. I was not expecting to see you quite yet, but this encounter is nonetheless delicious. How does it feel to be so distant, so powerless? Horrible, would you say? Now you understand what it was like for me, watching you, barely an adolescent, revered and adored by the entire simpering kingdom."

Carol stared at the siren she had believed to be her friend. "Oh, Mihuah, what have you done?"

"She has helped her beloved, human girl. Helped her people, her kingdom, her species. It was not so difficult, though. You are all rather foolish and gullible. Easily beguiled and deceived. And now you cannot stop what has begun."

Johnny rushed at the mirror as if he could dash through it.

"I wouldn't count us out yet, you freaking jerk."

Maxaltic laughed, gesturing at someone beyond the edges of the image. A hand appeared, passing a small rectangle to the rogue prince.

"Your bravado is meaningless. I shall do what I please. Take what I want. And you will simply despair. Do you recognize this, orphans?"

Maxaltic held the object up to the mirror.

It was their father's passport card.

Carol felt herself die inside.

"No!" raged Johnny, slamming his fist against the wall.

"Yes," Maxaltic answered smugly. Then he reached toward them, and the mirror went blank.

Carol, though broken, found the strength to whirl on Mihuah.

"You betrayed us! The jellyfish, the explosion, the sharks— that was all you. And you made sure we came here, didn't you? You piece of…Are my parents dead? Does he have the Shadow Stone?"

Mihuah set her jaw tightly and said nothing.

"Answer her, damn it!" Johnny shouted, lifting the staff.

Ana thrust herself between them. "No, Johnny, not like this! She is my cousin. Let me talk to her. I can reach her."

Carol could almost hear Tezcatlipoca laughing. *You are a wolf at heart, and when the time comes, you will rip what you require from your enemies.*

Pulling Ana out of the way, she muttered, "There's not enough time for that."

She reached out, yanked away a curl of Mihuah's short, rusty hair.

Then she assumed the siren's shape and dove deep into her memories.

Maxaltic had found her in her mother's office that day, less than a ceremonial year ago. Mihuah had been reviewing different politicians' positions, preparing to brief the minister for her talk to the Assembly. A smile had crossed her face as the prince entered.

"Ah, my love. Are you not concerned that an aid will see you and start some nasty rumor? I was promised to you from birth, but you know how the traditionalists will react."

Maxaltic had cupped her head with his hand for a moment. Then shadows had seemed to creep across his eyes.

"Indeed. Sadly, my mother the Queen will soon make an announcement that will quash any such speculation, Mihuah."

"What? Your expression concerns me, sweet. Why do you hesitate?"

His jaw had twisted with barely bridled rage. "She has been working to deepen our alliance with Qucha Llaqta. The idea is that I shall marry the eldest princess, uniting the two realms and solidifying the Queen's hegemony in Eastern Apan."

Mihuah's pulse had quickened, nausea spreading through her belly. "But...no! You and I are *betrothed*, Maxaltic! Why would she choose to dilute the blood of the House of Napotza?"

"Because she hungers for power, as well you know."

A low moan had escaped Mihuah's lips. Then the prince had kissed her.

"Soft, beloved. I have merely explained my mother's plans. I shall see myself damned before I marry anyone other than you, Mihuah. As much as I, too, wish to ensure the ascendency of Tapachco in these seas, the Queen's path is not the only one available to us."

Getting her emotions in check, letting the diplomat in her take control, Mihuah had asked, "What do you mean?"

"Recently an elemental appeared to me, my love, and

showed me how I might not only raise Tapachco to the greatness of millennia past, but also dominate the Five Nations and the entire world. Humanity has grown dangerous, it told me. At any moment, our fragile freedom from their corrosive ways could end. Yet I have been chosen, the Lord of Water announced, by the gods themselves to wield the might of the Shadow Stone."

Mihuah had found herself unable to speak, instead simply shaking her head unbelievingly.

"It is no myth, beloved. I had that wench, my sister, perform a Retelling to confirm the elemental's words. And though believed lost, that fell device is within reach. My distant cousin Celic, once Royal Historian and monk, has walked among human beings for several years now, searching. He will be my guide, opening a passage way for the army that the Lords of Water will help me to assemble."

Drawing her close to him, Maxaltic had enfolded Mihuah into a warm embrace, his forehead pressed against her own.

"But I cannot be followed, beloved. The Royal Guard and the court sorcerers must be somehow distracted, drawn off after a red herring."

It had taken a moment for Mihuah to understand.

"Me. You wish me to aid you in this distraction." Her heart fluttering madly in her chest, she had squeezed him closer. "Very well, my love. Tell me what I must do."

⌐◙◙◙◙◙◙◙◙◙⌐

Carol shook herself free of that specific memory as all the rest rushed into her awareness. Bringing forward her features and voice, she turned to the others.

"She was in cahoots with him from the beginning. Her job was to keep us off his trail while Celic tricked Dad and his friends into opening up the apiyaztli in El Chanal."

A look of shocked understanding crossed Johnny's face. "Oh, crap. Don Cecilio, the old dude who told the archaeologists about the tunnels!"

"Yes. Celic, in human form. Mihuah also knew we were coming because Celic spun a half-truth for the Little People. All she had to do was come along for the ride, nudging us in the right direction if we got off the false track."

Anamacani looked as if she might die of sorrow. "Oh, dear cousin, how could you? Carol, did she truly attempt to kill us?"

There was no more hiding from reality. Carol had little desire to soften the blow.

"Yes, she did. In his years searching for the stone, Celic had come across the waystation and explored it pretty thoroughly. That knowledge was passed to Maxaltic, who told Mihuah what she needed to do to make sure we didn't foil his plans."

Ana crumpled in despair. Johnny reached for her, tried to give her a little comfort while keeping the staff pointed at the traitor.

There's no time for this, Carol shot at him.

I know. I know.

"Twins."

They both looked over at Jabalí, who had called to them softly in his harsh tongue. No longer was he squeezing his head in agony. Instead, he tapped a webbed finger against his temple.

"I remember now. Other things. The Shadow Stone lies in the depths of the pool where I taught those children how to swim, so long ago. Jabalí Lagoon. Not far from the temple at El Chanal. There we hid it, and for ages it was guarded by sentinels loyal to the Lord of Creation. I was the last. A century ago a Lord of Water arrived and strove with me, trying to wrest the device away. I nearly succumbed, Carol and Johnny. Yet some powerful being aided me, dispelling the elemental. Sadly, my mind was shattered. I no longer knew who I was or what I did. I emerged into the sun and air, I spent a few weeks among the humans, and then—forgive me, friends—I abandoned the stone."

Carol felt despair, thick like shadow magic, curl itself around her heart.

"All this time, it was sitting right there. We left Dad in the hands of the enemy, Johnny, and dragged ourselves off to the bottom of the ocean for nothing."

Releasing Ana, her brother grabbed her in a shuddering hug.

"Don't give up, Carol. We still have the apiyaztli."

"You don't get it, do you? Elementals just came through it. The thing leads to Tlalocan. It won't do us any good, Johnny. We've lost."

Mihuah, eyes still warily glancing at the staff, gave a disgusted laugh. Johnny cocked his head at her menacingly, and she fell silent.

"No," he said. "That's what Tezcatlipoca wants us to think. But Xolotl promised, Carol. So we're going to try, do you hear me?"

She heard him, alright. She also heard the echo of another, darker voice.

Are you ready, child? It is now your turn. Let us see how far you can be bent, Carolina.

CHAPTER NINETEEN

Things couldn't get much uglier. Johnny had Jabalí seize Mihuah, and they left the chamber to meet up with Marshal Cenaman, who had a hard time believing that the siren she had watched over as a child could betray their trust so completely. She even seemed to doubt the word of the princess. But when Mihuah finally spoke, there was no avoiding the truth.

"Enough of your insipid prattling. I did what was necessary to preserve the prince and the realm."

Cenaman, clearly heart-broken, remanded her into the custody of one of her captains, who bound her and led her out of the temple to be held under guard along with Tenamic until they could return to Tapachco and stand trial for their treachery.

The marshal looked over the miserable civilians. "I must call together my command staff. If you cannot find a passageway out of Atlan, we must devise some other strategy."

She swam away, leaving them with a small squad of guards.

"Carol," Johnny called. "Ana. Jabalí. Come on."

They swam into the inner sanctum. Ana looked dejectedly up at the statue of the goddess.

"I cannot bear much more," she whispered, as if in prayer.

Carol had withdrawn into herself and said nothing. Only

Jabalí radiated any form of positive energy, almost jittering with excitement.

"Touch the mirror again, Johnny," the tlacamichin urged.

"I don't know, dude. Last time I did that, I freaking conjured up a trio of angry elementals. There's got to be another way."

He thought back to his vision of Xolotl, recalling the massive dog's final words as he had faded away. A surge of hope brought a smile to his lips. He wheeled to regard his sister.

"Carol, look at me."

Her despondent eyes came up to meet his.

"Remember the Well of Souls in Mictlan? Remember the song that only you could hear?"

His sister's lips began to tremble.

"Sing, Carol. Sing it for me, please."

Hugging her arms against her chest, she hesitated a moment as if searching inside herself for the melody or for the strength to push despair away.

Then she opened her mouth, and the most beautiful music Johnny had ever heard came streaming out, wordless yet filled with promise; unearthly harmonies in a voice that blended human girl, siren, tlacamichin, goddess.

The song worked its magic on them all. Johnny felt his anger and fear drop away, replaced by a sure courage and replenished love. Ana turned to stare at Carol, her face lit up by wonder and relief. The guards who had followed them straightened their dejected backs, glancing at each other with renewed purpose.

And Jabalí spun around, excited beyond stillness, crying, "I remember who I am! I know my name! By the beloved goddess *I KNOW MY NAME!*"

The water above the mirror had begun to roil and spin. Suddenly inspired, Johnny called, "Say it, Jabalí! Say your name!"

"Rikar Tzaaq, Johnny. I am Rikar Tzaaq. 'Precious scale.' So did my hatch father name me two centuries ago."

Johnny reached out to the mirror with savage magic as his sister's song swelled louder and louder.

We need a path to the lagoon where Rikar Tzaaq once guarded the Shadow Stone. Someone, please. This is the hour of our greatest need.

"I hear you, Juan Ángel Garza. And I hear you as well, Carolina Garza. I had not hoped to hear the Hymn of Duality again until my long days had come to an end."

Surging from the surface of the mirror came the most beautiful woman Johnny had ever seen, a looming giant of a siren with human features, her tail obscured by the shimmering green skirt that seemed to flow forever in streams of living emerald.

It was Matlalcueyeh, the goddess of the sea, crowned with writhing blue electric eels. Around her neck hung a coral yoke studded with glowing aquamarine gems, bright against a blouse the hue of deep ocean water.

Ana and the guards immediately bowed their heads. Rikar Tzaaq laughed with ecstatic delight. Johnny and Carol, who had stood in the presence of gods before, looked up at Matlalcueyeh expectantly.

"I see the lingering doubt in your souls, my children. Fear not. Your parents are alive. As they are both near water, I am able to sense them. Indeed, I have tarried in my appearance here precisely because I strove to succor them, sending the *Encante* to the side of each."

Johnny thought back to his vision. "The Encante? Are those

the pink dolphins Xolotl showed me?"

"Yes, Juan Ángel. They are the least numerous of the Blessed Creatures, wise river dwellers able to assume human form when needed, but their fealty to me is undying and strong. For the better part of a century, they have aided me by keeping a silent vigil over the Shadow Stone."

Carol, clearly calmed and comforted by the song she had sung, nonetheless shook her head in confusion at this news.

"Wait—if you knew where it was, why didn't anyone tell us? Why did we have to go through this horror?"

"Ah, child. Keeping it hidden from some required keeping it hidden from all. When a group of tlacamichimeh called out to me centuries ago, entreating my aid as they sought to foil the dark plans of Tezcatlipoca, I found I could not refuse, not only because of the suffering Tezcatlipoca caused me during the Fourth Age of this world, but also because their design was noble and good. So we spirited the device to a distant lagoon, and I enshrouded it with all the magic I could muster. Afterward, I could not risk revealing its location to other gods for fear my husband would learn what I had done and report to the loathsome Lord of Chaos."

Rikar Tzaaq approached her, webbed hands clasped before him. "Mother of the Seas, for your many boons I offer thanks on behalf of my people. But, though my memory has been restored, I do not fully comprehend what happened to make me abandon my post."

"Rest assured it was no fault of yours, my child. A century ago, one of Tlaloc's elemental children chanced to follow me as I traveled to ensure your good health and the Shadow Stone's safety. That Lord of Water attacked, nearly destroying you before I could imprison him. For decades Tlaloc searched for his lost son. When he finally discovered and freed him not many years ago, my husband and his dark master began this sinister plot you have found yourselves caught up in. Since then, I have been carefully watched, until Juan Ángel's touch on the emerald mirror drew my guards away."

Carol nodded, but didn't seem completely convinced. "That explains why you didn't say anything, but I find it hard to believe that Quetzalcoatl couldn't see the stone. Why would he let the Little People believe Celic's lie?"

Johnny reached out, touched her arm. "Sis, you already know that he wants us to make our own decisions and stuff. The whole free will thing. Annoying, yeah, but..."

Matlalcueyeh floated free of the mirror, reduced her size to move closer to the twins.

"I cannot speak for my elder brother, but it is true that he learned long ago the price of meddling too closely with the affairs of the Blessed Creatures. I suspect that, if he knowingly allowed you to be deceived, it was to bring you here. You have destroyed the Apixqueh, releasing me from Tlaloc's control. Thus have I returned to this temple after long millennia, ready to give you a most precious gift."

The goddess extended a glowing hand and touched Johnny's chest. He could sense a bit of her divinity detach itself and cling to the cloak of Huitzilopochtli. She turned to Carol and did the same.

"You need to use apiyaztli to travel to your parents. This is easily done. Unlike the smoking mirrors you have used, our tunnels are not limited to one exit point. Fix the destination in your mind. See it clearly. Then step into the eddy above the mirror, and you will be drawn to it."

Johnny grinned. "A snap, huh? But I think I hear a catch coming…"

"Indeed. Sacred tunnels pass through the realms of gods. The path you will access with this mirror, for instance, cuts through Tlalocan. If you had attempted to use that apiyaztli, you would have been seized by my husband or one of his sons."

"Not good, I'm guessing." Johnny felt his natural sarcasm returning. It was good to be more or less back to normal.

"No. But now I have marked you both with my sigil. You will not be sensed as you make your way through Tlalocan."

You hear that, Carol? Stealth mode, baby.

Ha. Can you give me a little more time to recover before you start with your corny jokes?

A smile lit up the face of the goddess so brightly that they had to avert their eyes.

"Humor is the path to joy, which reminds us of our love."

"Oops. She can read our minds, Sis."

Carol gave a weak laugh. "Well, she is a goddess, doofus."

"Lovely, children. Lovely. Now it is time for you to depart. I am afraid that a difficult choice lies before you. Your father and the Encante, at this very moment, are assailed by Maxaltic and his forces. Meanwhile, my husband has learned of my escape. He has sent some of his sons against your mother and the men aboard that ship."

Johnny turned to Carol. "Where do we go first?"

She bit her lip. "Well, the Shadow Stone is the most danger-ous thing we've got to deal with."

"Yeah, but I've already seen what's going to happen to Mom. She won't last long."

Pulling nervously at her braids, Carol groaned. "If we go to her, how do we get to Jabalí Lagoon? There's no emerald mirror on the *Estela de Mar*."

Matlalcueyeh made a calming gesture.

"The mirrors merely stabilize the sacred tunnels, children. Gods can create their own passageways, though these swiftly fade. To surround your mother, the tlaloqueh have opened such a temporary apiyaztli. It may be that, upon rescuing your mother, you could gain access to it before it disappears."

"How?" Johnny asked. "If there's no mirror, how do we see it?"

"You must see through the eyes of your tonal. The sacred tunnel will be resplendent with teotl."

Carol gritted her teeth. "There's no guarantee that we'll get Mom quick enough to use the elemental's passageway. I don't know, Johnny. It means risking the lives of everyone."

He frowned in irritation. "I'm not leaving Mom to fend for herself, Carol. If you want to go to Dad first, well…maybe we should split up. You take the guards and go to Jabalí Lagoon. I'll go get Mom and meet you there."

She nodded. "Okay, then. That might work."

"Sadly, you cannot take more than one other person with you, twins." Matlalcueyeh gestured at the glittering eddy. "It is time. Take whomever you choose by both hands and enter the mirror. I will tend to the needs of the merfolk who remain."

Carol asked Rikar Tzaaq, "Will you come with me?"

The tlacamichin's froggy lips spread in a smile. "Yes, Carol."

Johnny was about to say something, but his sister took the fish-man's webbed hands in hers and dove toward the emerald without another word.

"Okay," he muttered to himself, picturing his mother, running up and down the deck of the *Estela de Mar* in jaguar form. "Here goes nothing."

A hand fell on his shoulder.

"Hold."

It was Ana. Her fingers found his, and her left palm enfolding his right, which gripped Tenamic's staff. Wild electric blue dreads danced around them both as she pulled him close, pressing her forehead against his.

"You will not leave without me, Johnny Garza. I must stand with you against my brother and the forces that would destroy both our peoples."

Swallowing hard as he looked deeply into her eyes, his chest tightening with unexpected emotions, he managed to mutter, "Alrighty, then."

And he pulled the beautiful siren with him into the unknown.

CHAPTER TWENTY

The membrane between worlds stretched and tore, sending Carol and Rikar Tzaaq hurtling through a tube of translucent green energy. Their passage took them soaring through misty skies above a watery landscape, something akin to a bayou or rain forest, veined with rivers and dotted with lakes. On the horizon a lush, green mountain rose impossibly high, its summit wreathed in clouds that allowed only a glimpse of a massive jade palace.

Tlalocan. One of the four possible destinations of the dead in the old religion.

Thunder rumbled, muffled by distance or the apiyaztli. Skeins of lightning webbed the clouds. Carol thought she saw the green, blue and yellow glow of elementals moving here and there in the sky and in the water.

"Let us pray we are not detected," Rikar Tzaaq breathed.

"Right? That'd be a big mess for everyone."

She closed her eyes to better focus on the face of her father, on the water and trees that had surrounded Maxaltic in the obsidian mirror earlier. The tunnel appeared to dip, perhaps to climb, maybe to twist in a direction her mind was unable to understand.

Then, with a rush of shifting pressure, they burst forth into the shallows at the edge of a broad lagoon. Carol assumed her normal human form and looked around.

Trees ringed the glassy expanse: tall pines, twisted red cedar and heavy live oak. Beyond them, still exhaling wisps of smoke, stood the Volcán de Colima like an eager sentinel keeping a vigil over the many lakes hidden in its foothills.

"You look very different, Carol," Rikar Tzaaq said.

She glanced down at her light brown hands and arms.

"Yeah, I guess I do, huh? Feels strange to be in my own skin."

A noise to their left caused them to pivot.

Carol gasped.

Twenty meters away, her father stood in water up to his chest. He brandished a dark wooden staff as if preparing for attack. A group of pink dolphins swam in protective circles around him.

Oscar Garza and the Encante were surrounded by a hundred armed tritons and tlacamichimeh, weapons at the ready.

"Dad!" Carol shouted, splashing her way toward the stand-off.

Several of the warriors spun to face her and her companion.

"Carol?" Her father raised a hand to block the afternoon glare. "Careful! Where's Johnny?"

"Getting Mom. They'll be here soon."

She came to a stop, sizing up her options. Johnny had explained how to get her tonal to dredge up past forms without any DNA, and she thought back to the creatures she had become during the last six months.

"You need to watch out, *m'ija*! They're just waiting on Maxaltic. He and don Cecilio—who's a merman, if you can believe it—went down through a channel into a chamber that lies under the lagoon. That's where the Shadow Stone really is, apparently. But the Encante—that's these sentient dolphins here—tell me it's well protected by the glamor of some goddess."

"Matlalcueyeh. Yes, she's the one who helped me get back to you this fast, Dad. I know about Cecilio—he's really Celic, a crazy atacatl who can shapeshift into human form. Have they hurt you at all?"

Oscar Garza shook his head. "Nope. See, I found the scepter of Epan Napotza. It's a really powerful artifact, it seems. These guys are pretty scared of it."

"It's a nahualcuahuitl, Dad—a sorcerer's staff. That one was carved from a piece of the World Tree by elementals thousands of years ago."

"That's what the Encante said. They taught me an incantation for using it. Another reason for this little stand-off."

One of the guards nearest to Carol made a cutting gesture with his hand. "That's enough of this babbling," he barked in Nahuatl. "We can't have the enemy making plans in some barbaric tongue right in front of us!"

Carol had been thinking about diving deep to go after Maxaltic, but that would have left her father exposed. Now this atlacatl's linguistic confusion gave her another idea. Catching the attention of a close-by tlacamichin, she called to him in his language.

"So, do you enjoy having these scale-less mermen give you orders? What weak-webbed shoal did you come from to enter into such a disgusting alliance?"

Rikar Tzaaq caught on right away.

"Indeed. What self-respecting son of the deep would treat

these slick-skinned abominations as clutch-mates? I suspect you will learn to regret this embarrassing alliance when their prince returns with his prize and burns you to a crisp."

The tlacamichimeh began to twitch in agitation, and the atlacah leveled weapons at them, cautious looks on their faces.

The guard who had spoken a moment before now made a short leap in Carol's direction. "What're you saying to each other, meddlesome girl?"

"Why? Are you worried they'll betray you?" She shifted into a siren, diving into the water near him and twittering in the merfolk tongue. "Maxaltic and Celic haven't returned yet because the gilled fiends were waiting for them down below. You're all fools for allying with your oldest enemy."

Chaos erupted. Long centuries of hatred had been barely repressed for this dark mission, so those animosities quickly spiraled into violence. Atlacah and tlacamichimeh grappled in the pristine water, exchanging blows with fists and weapons.

"Keep away, Rikar," she commanded before turning her thoughts inward, calling to her tonal.

Remember this shape? The second you ever assumed? I need you to fly. You know you want to feel the wind beneath us. Come on!

Carol leaped into the air and became a *kamasotz*, a snatch-bat from the bowels of Mictlan. Beating black wings fiercely, she rose higher and higher, rotating her vulpine head to scan the in-fighting aquatic beings with keen red eyes. Then she dropped, the wind ruffling the gold fur at her neck as she aimed the cruel black talons of her feet at an unsuspecting merman, seizing him and lifting him thirty meters before releasing him. Smashing against the surface of the lagoon, he rolled unconscious into its depths.

Pleased at the enraged response from those below, Carol grabbed several more tritons and man-fish and flung them back down one by one, easily avoiding the missiles launched her way by the startled warriors.

But the water at the center of the lagoon began to roil. Carol wheeled about in a spiral, waiting, ready to defend her father at all costs.

Leaping from the water with a triumphant shout, came Prince Maxaltic.

Held high in his right hand was an uneven ball of ambergris, its mottled grays and browns flashing like the wet hide of a diseased frog.

Even from this distance, Carol could feel the thick and silent blackness curling in its center, eager to be released after eight hundred centuries of waiting.

In Cehuallocozcatl. The Shadow Stone.

"Behold!" Maxaltic cried, and the struggling warriors stopped to look. "At a great cost, the life of my blood-kin Celic, I have retrieved the direst weapon this age has ever known. Today we purge the world of humanity, brothers and friends. Today I bring a deluge the cosmos will not soon forget."

Before she could dive toward the prince, her father lifted the ancient staff.

"No, you will not!" he shouted. Closing his eyes, he muttered in an arcane language. The runes on the scepter of Epan Napotza glowed blood red, and a gout of ruddy fire burst from its tip, scorching the air before slamming into the Shadow Stone.

Incredibly, Maxaltic managed to keep his grip on the device, pushing forward with kicks of his tail, allowing the energy to be absorbed.

The stone began to react. Tendrils of inky smoke curled around Maxaltic's hand and arm. The air was soon a-thrum with terrible power that rattled the trees and sent waves splashing against the pines.

Oscar Garza's eyes were closed. He kept muttering the incantation, pouring greater and greater force into the Shadow Stone.

Carol suddenly understood.

This is what sank Atlan. Quelel came at Epan, and he tried to counter her attack. But the stone sucked up the energy and detonated, destroying everything they loved. And now Tezcatlipoca has engineered all this so that the staff and stone will clash again. Dad's going to cause a cataclysm. He's going to get himself and a lot of others killed.

Without further thought, Carol dipped toward her father, grabbing his shirt and spinning him off balance. His hands slipped from the staff, and she grabbed it, climbing an updraft and winging over toward Rikar Tzaaq.

"Keep this from them!" she managed to screech.

The Shadow Stone was still humming, though. Maxaltic gripped it in both hands, exulting at the ribbons of sable force that twisted outward from its bleak center.

I've got to destroy it.

Plunging toward the water, Carol shifted into her gigantic squid form, shooting out tentacles to fling warriors away from her dazed father and to rip the Shadow Stone from Maxaltic's fingers.

Ignoring the silence that began to ooze into her mind, she squeezed with all her might. Though she poured savage magic into her sinews, it wasn't quite enough. Frantic, her tonal sought to help her, bringing forward human characteristics until the tentacle became a massive fist, crushing the ancient ball of verdigris by slow degrees.

But like spiritual venom, the shadow magic penetrated her defenses, worming its way into her soul, flooding her with darkness and cold and cruel quiet.

Then, like the fingers of a puppeteer, the black tendrils began to move her body, dragging it through the lagoon toward her father.

Carol could not stop herself. She was no longer in control.

And then Tezcatlipoca spoke within her mind.

"Do you see how utterly you are my creature, girl? Once again you have walked the path that I designed for you, eagerly entering the trap, damned by your own laudable purpose. Now you hold the key to apocalypse in your hand, and together you and I shall rip open the cosmos to bring an end to all you love."

Why...

"Ah, you are too overcome to even form the words, but I can see your question. Why have I never availed myself of the Shadow Stone before? Why formulate such an elaborate ruse to put it in your mighty fist? Come, girl. Setting aside the fact that my idiot brother has managed to seal the earth from my direct presence, do you really think I would leave such a tool to lie dormant for millennia if I could use it myself to end the world? Shadow magic I possess aplenty, but it does not suffice. The Shadow Stone, however, can amplify *savage* magic, and only one of your ilk can wield it on the scale that I require."

The Lord of Chaos made her stop. She loomed above her father.

Never...

"Oh, you shall indeed channel your xoxal into this device, Carolina Garza. Your despair at killing your father will leave you no other recourse."

Slowly, pulling against Carol's every effort to stop him, laughing at the inner howling of her tonal, Tezcatlipoca lifted her tentacle high into the air, preparing to beat Oscar Garza to death with fist and stone and magic.

Cowering in the shallows, her father lifted his hands as if to ward off her blows. A few of the Encante shifted into humanoid form, surrounding him, pink arms outstretched.

"No, Sweetie! You have to fight it!"

But Carol was being shoved down, deeper and deeper inside herself. His voice a faint echo, a fading memory.

Then a growl filled her awareness. Images began to flash.

Xolotl, bearing the twins across the river Chignahuapan at the edge of Mictlan.

A tall, slender god with bright green and blue feathers instead of hair, his skin highlighted in places by delicate golden scales.

Quetzalcoatl, Carol whispered.

The she saw the two of them, side by side, gathering bones in the darkness of the Underworld, ready to remake humanity by any means possible.

The growl came again, louder. Then the memory of conversations.

Tenamic's voice: "*In certain special individuals—Air Sages and naguales, for instance—this develops into a partly independent twin of our spirit.*"

"*Like my tonal,*" Carol had said.

"*Precisely. And the tonalli, given enough time—centuries, millennia—can acquire its own personality, as in the case of the gods.*"

Ana's voice: "*Though you should both be jaguars, Carol has been gifted with a wolf tonal for a reason we cannot perceive. As for me, I trust in the wisdom of the gods.*"

Carol could feel Tezcatlipoca pull her tentacle as high as it would go. She could hear his horrible burbling laughter pouring from the mouth of the giant squid.

The growl in her inner darkness became a snarl.

We're bound together in this form.

...**yes**...

The voice was rough and bestial.

But we don't have to be.

...**no**...

I can let you free. His hold will be broken. Dad will be safe. The world won't be destroyed.

There was no more answer, just expectant panting and a strange clawing at her heart. An eager whine, like a dog makes when it wants to burst from its master's home.

And deep within the darkness, Carol smiled, reaching for the door.

CHAPTER TWENTY ONE

Because of the odd weight of the staff, Johnny and Ana tumbled awkwardly for a while in the dizzying rush of the apiyaztli, but they eventually stabilized. Tlalocan spread beneath them, luxurious and dark, like an uncharted jungle full of deadly beauty.

"His jade palace sits atop the mountain," Ana whispered. "See the bolts of lightning that flash through the clouds? Those are some of his sons. The rest, the stories tell us, abide in the streams, rivers and lakes of this realm, attending the souls who dwell here and awaiting his bidding."

"Or keeping his wife prisoner."

Ana gave an exasperated smile. "That as well."

The sacred tunnel made an unexpected, twisty turn, diving into a swamp and once more through the barrier between worlds. Then, with a rushing splash of sea water bursting into air, the two were spewed sprawling onto the deck of the *Estela de Mar*.

Shifting back to his human form, Johnny leapt to his feet, brandishing Tenamic's staff. The yacht was rocking back and forth violently, and a large jaguar skidded by him, thrown off balance by a concussion of power against the stern.

"Mom?"

She snarled at him, jerking her feline head at the ocean. Three blue-gemmed Lords of Water were aiming strange canon of water and energy at the ship, preparing for another volley. Pink dolphins, part of the Encante, leapt at the elementals, slapping their tails against the beings' fluid limbs and frustrating their attack.

Still, one of the elementals managed to send a ball of crackling electricity caroming along the hull of the yacht. Sparks danced over the railing, falling on Verónica Quintero de Garza and making her yelp in pain.

Johnny lifted the sorcerer's staff and thrust it angrily toward the sea. "Leave my mother alone, freaks!"

He was more aware of himself this time, pouring xoxal into the runes on the staff, feeling that savage magic being channeled along the length of ancient ivory to explode in an unfocused, erratic beam from the thicker knob at its end.

Though he couldn't control his attack or narrow it in any way, Johnny waved the staff back and forth, pummeling first one and then another of the tlaloqueh. The Encante quickly dove to avoid his wild volley of power.

Sensing a weakening in the elementals, Johnny pointed his spitting ray of energy at just one of them, stripping away its watery flesh and cracking the gem within before turning to its brothers to do the same. The staff grew hotter and hotter, but he ignored the searing of his own skin, his grim expression twisting into a shout of rage and pain as he pounded the last Lord of Water with magic that grew exponential, making the air itself crackle and hum with violence.

As the last elemental gem shattered, so did the staff, slicing Johnny's arms with shards of petrified bone.

In the sudden absence of his attack, the sea was unnaturally quiet and calm.

"¡Ay, dios mío, Juan Ángel!"

It was his mother. She had shifted back to human form and was wearing a simple sundress. Beside her, worry clouding her now human face, stood Ana. Behind them, emerging from below decks, came Captain Sandoval and his sons.

"It's okay, Mom. I'm not hurt that bad."

He shifted briefly to a jaguar and back to speed his healing. She speedily crossed the deck to enfold him in her arms, burying her face in his chest.

"That's not what scares me, *m'ijo*. What did you just do? How? That was terrifying!"

Ana touched her reassuringly. "Do not be concerned, madam," she said in Spanish. "This is the staff of a sorcerer. Johnny and Carol used it before to defeat a group of elementals. It seems that they use it better together than singly."

"Who are you? And where is my Carolina, Johnny? Tell me she's okay."

"Carol's okay, Mom, though maybe not for long. And this is Princess Anamacani of Tapachco. Ana, this is my mother, Verónica Quintero de Garza."

"I am honored, Lady Verónica."

Johnny's mother smiled slightly at the title.

"Likewise, Your Highness."

Captain Sandoval, realizing who was standing on his deck, dropped to his knees and gestured for his sons to do the same.

"Long live the House of Napotza!" he declared in a shaky voice.

Ana gave the salute of her people, both palms first pressed to the forehead, then a wide and sweeping gesture with the arms.

"Tapochca thanks you for your service, sir."

Verónica raised an eyebrow at Johnny and smirked. "She's a little old for you, no?" she asked pointedly in English.

"Oh, my God, Mom, don't you start, too!" he whispered.

"Okay, okay. Just looking out for my son, you know. Not a crime, is it?"

Johnny sighed dramatically.

"No time for this right now. We've got to go. Dad's in danger, and Carol is trying to deal with it by herself."

Before his mother could respond, a pink-skinned creature leapt from the sea onto the deck beside them. Captain Sandoval stood, unholstering his pistol, but Johnny gestured for him to hold.

The newcomer rather startlingly resembled a human woman, and Verónica quickly handed her a towel to wrap around her.

"I am Botaben," she lilted in strange Spanish, "node leader for this bit of the Encante. That was very well done, human. Tell me, what more can we do to fulfill the command of the goddess that we defend your node?"

"Well, Botaben, my mother and I have to leave, now. But you could guide this ship back to port, if it's not too much to ask. The Sandovals have been through a lot, I figure, and I don't want any accidents to happen on their return trip."

"It will be done."

Johnny turned to Ana, whose brown skin glowed beautifully in the afternoon sunlight. "Can you stay for a while? Talk to the captain and explain what you can? His family deserves a second chance, Ana. And Tapachco needs a connection to the human world."

"Of course. I only wish I could accompany you and your mother."

"Yeah, I know. And I'd like it if we could talk some more, but the apiyaztli's probably already fading. I've got to go."

Swallowing hard, Ana nodded.

"Please, just...remember that Maxaltic is my brother. Protect our people, Johnny, but try to keep him safe as well, if you can."

An unexpected ache tightened his chest.

"Of course, Ana. I'll do my best. Good-bye, now."

"I suspect you are not ready for this," she muttered, "but I simply cannot resist." Leaning forward, she pressed her lips to his in a gentle kiss. "Goodbye, Johnny. I hope one day we may meet again."

Overcome by feelings he couldn't describe, unable to say anything in reply, he took his mother by the hand and called up his tonal, searching the water for signs of the tunnel.

There it sputtered weakly, just a few meters off the port side.

"Okay, Mom, grab both my hands."

He led her to the railing, and with a final glance back at the transformed siren and dolphin, they leapt into the sea.

The entrance was already closing. Johnny scrabbled at it with savage magic, wedging it open for an instant more.

"Hold your breath!" he shouted, and then he pulled his mother into the apiyaztli with him.

This time the shortcut through Tlalocan took them directly over the sprawling jade palace that crowned the mountain at the center of the realm. Johnny could see that it was circular, like

Mictlan, with concentric rings of different vegetation, including a broad river that separated the mountain from the rest of the paradise.

Then the tunnel lifted, boring into clouds and beyond into the physical plane.

Johnny and his mother sprawled into wet earth at the edge of Jabali Lagoon. Looming like a nightmare above them was a twisted, mammoth merging of squid and human. It clutched one fist high in the air, and from between those massive fingers black tendrils of shadow magic curled, twining along the tentacles and burrowing into the monster's eyes.

Below it lay Johnny's father, hands raised in supplication, surrounded by human-shifted members of the Encante.

All around sprawled the unconscious bodies of atlacah and tlacamichimeh.

"No, Sweetie!" Oscar Garza screamed. "You have to fight it!"

"Oh, dear Mother of God, it's Carol!" Johnny's mother cried, rushing to his aid.

The lagoon bubbled and echoed with dark laughter, familiar to Johnny despite coming from a squid's mouth beneath the surface.

Tezcatlipoca had possessed his sister.

"Johnny!" came a familiar, gurgling voice. Standing in the water just beyond Carol's monstrous form was Rikar Tzaaq, brandishing a staff. Johnny understood immediately that this was the scepter of Epan Napotza, perhaps the only tool on earth capable of destroying the Shadow Stone.

While his mother struggled to drag his father away from danger, aided by the Encante, Johnny ran toward the tlacamichin, determined to save his sister by shattering the ball of verdigris in her hand.

Before he could reach the staff a figure leapt from the water to seize him and drag him under. Maxaltic's hands went round Johnny's neck like a noose.

He shrugged and shifted into glowing, deep sea plankton long enough to escape the prince's grasp, then became a tlacamichin and dragged him out of the water, holding him with a single webbed hand.

"Really, you jealous punk? You're going to pick a fight with a nagual?"

Maxaltic spat in his face.

"Oh, you did *not* just go there, dude. Alright, this is for Anamacani, you freak. She deserved a better brother than you."

Johnny curled his other scaly hand into a fist and punched the prince right in the jaw, knocking him completely out.

Rikar Tzaaq had reached his side, and extended the staff.

"I shall watch over him, Johnny. Go save your family. Go save us all."

Johnny grabbed the staff, nodded and turned.

The fist was coming down.

His mother and father were in its path.

"No, Carolina, *¡no lo hagas!*" screamed Verónica in frantic fear.

Johnny lifted the staff, trying to sense the stone in his sister's hand.

And then the strangest thing happened. The monstrosity simply collapsed with a thunderous clap and flash of light. The Shadow Stone tumbled into the mud not far from his parents, rolling to a squelching stop at their feet.

Standing unexpectedly in the shallows were Carol—the Robe of Mayahuel draped loosely over her long limbs—and a large wolf, its yellow-gray pelt and black markings a familiar sight.

For a moment, no one said a word.

Carol broke the stunned silence with a laugh. Reaching out to rub the wolf's head, she shouted, "Hey, everybody, I'd like you to meet my tonal!"

Johnny shook his head, incredulous. "No. Freaking. Way. Dude! You can split into two? That is totally *not fair!*"

He ran to his sister and wrapped his arms around her.

"He almost got me," she whispered in his ear. "Almost bent me to his will, Johnny. But we're not alone. No matter how bad things get, we've got allies. We've got family. We've got each other."

The wolf nuzzled in between the two of them, looking up at Johnny with eyes he'd seen many times before.

...and...you have...us...

The jaguar stirred within him, joyous at the snarling voice. His parents came stumbling over, and the whole Garza family fell together in a tearful embrace.

When they at last pulled away from each other, the Encante and Rikar Tzaaq stood, waiting expectantly.

"There is still one more task for you, my friends," the tlacamichin said, the Nahuatl words harsh in his gilled throat.

He gestured at the Shadow Stone, which was sinking deep into the mire at the edge of the lagoon, as if trying to slip away from them and save itself for greater mayhem.

Johnny looked at the scepter in his hands and glanced at his sister.

"What do you say, Carol? Want to play ball?"

She smiled and crooked a finger at her tonal, which crouched down and jumped at her, going insubstantial at the last second and burrowing into her chest. Her eyes went yellow for a second; then she shrugged the loose gown into jeans and a t-shirt.

"Heck, yes," she said, laying her hands on the staff near his.

Their father cleared his throat as they took aim.

"Um, kids? Are you sure that's safe?"

Johnny looked over at him and gave a little shrug.

"Nothing's safe, Dad. But that's okay. We got this."

And their animal selves rushed eagerly down their arms and into the carved bit of the World Tree, howling together in feral glee as they blasted the ancient verdigris to ash with waves of savage magic.

CODA

A few days later, Carol lay back on the sand, staring up at the star-studded darkness over the Pacific. Regional music echoed loudly all around as revelers prepared themselves for New Year's traditions and celebrations.

Her mother dropped a bag on the towel beside her and sat down with a sigh. "Well, I finally found grapes, though they cost me an arm and a leg. *Aprovechados.*"

"Where's Dad and Johnny? It's almost midnight."

"Well, *el menso de tu hermano* insisted on going back to the hotel to get his tablet. I swear, you millennials and your technology…"

Carol laughed, "You know what he's waiting for, Mom."

"Yeah, but I'm his mother. You can't fault me for being over-protective of his heart."

Thudding steps came louder and louder, and the two Garza men dashed toward them across the sand, racing each other.

"Oh, look, Mom. How cute! Dad thinks he can still beat Johnny in something physical."

"Shhh. Don't let him hear you. Mid-life crisis *y todo eso.*"

Johnny and Dr. Garza collapsed on their towels beside Carol and her mother, breathing heavily.

"That's cutting it pretty close, guys," Carol scolded them.

"Was it at least worth it, Johnny?"

"Yeah. She had Saúl Sandoval—the youngest, remember?—send an email with a video attachment."

Verónica yanked at Johnny's tablet.

"Well, come on, let's see it. Unless...I don't know...it's too private?"

"*Ya basta, mamá*. That got old days ago. Hang on a second."

The screen flickered on, blinding them all for a moment. Then Johnny hit play on the video application, and the face of Princess Anamacani filled the screen. She was in human form, sitting on the shore of San Benedicto Island, being filmed by one of the Sandoval family members.

"Hello, Johnny and Carol. Greetings to your parents as well. As promised, I bring you news of the consequences of Maxaltic's rebellion. Rikar Tzaaq arrived safely among us, with my brother in custody. The prince is now awaiting trial along with Mihuah. The Encante brought as many of the rebel atlacah as possible to the shores of this island, and they are likewise imprisoned. We have seen no sign of the tlacamichimeh that escaped the battle of Jabalí Lagoon, but the Royal Guard remains ever watchful.

"Tenamic has recovered from the madness that drove him to attack you. Rikar Tzaaq conveyed to the Queen and King your desire that he not be prosecuted. He has been stripped of his authority and position, and he has expressed a wish to live out his days as an adept of the Order of the Deep.

"As for me, I am well, despite having lost my only brother and best friend to treachery, despite being separated now from my two new friends by so many rods of ocean."

Carol giggled. "Oh, I *bet* it's me that she misses."

"*Ya párale, loca,*" Johnny groaned, exasperated.

Sighing, Ana continued, "But my duty to my people is clear, as is yours to all Blessed Creatures. Perhaps we will once again join forces against dangers that threaten life beneath the waves and above them. Until then, remember me fondly, as I remember you."

Standing, she saluted the camera before leaping into the ocean and disappearing from view.

Carol saw the glisten in her brother's eye and decided not to tease him. Instead, she reached out and squeezed his hand.

"Come on. Check the time, Johnny."

He pulled up the clock.

"Oh, dude, one minute!"

Their mom frantically handed out twelve grapes to each member of the Garza family, firm believer in Mexican tradition that she was. As they counted down to the New Year, they plopped the plump spheres into their mouths, laughing at the juice that ran down their chins.

When the clock clicked to midnight, they hugged each other tight, shouting best wishes and expressions of affection over the blare of trumpets and sawing of violins on the boardwalk.

Then the sky was filled with fireworks, bright blossoms that lit the sky and sea. As her parents gave each other a sort of embarrassing kiss, Carol noticed Johnny slipping down to the water's edge. She followed him, leaning her head against his shoulder as he stared at the reflection of fire upon the water.

"We're two of the good ones, right?" he muttered.

"Of course we are. And you know why? *This.* Because *this* is what matters to us. Not power, not kingdoms—just you and me and the people we love, standing on a beach beneath fireworks and stars."

He smiled and wrapped his arm around her shoulder.

What a goofball. My sister, the nerdy poet. Happy New Year, Carol.

Happy New Year, Johnny.

In the distance, under the lingering traces of smoke, pink dolphins danced among the breaking waves.

The adventures of Johnny and Carol will continue in
THE HIDDEN CITY
GARZA TWINS: BOOK THREE
coming in 2017

GUIDE TO PRONUNCIATION

Words in Spanish and Nahuatl (the human language that the merfolk of Tapachco also speak) have pretty much similar pronunciation rules, so they are combined below.

Vowels

a—as in "father".

e—as in "bet".

i—as in "police".

o—as in "no".

u—as in "flute" (Spanish only).

Diphthongs (vowel combinations)

ai—like the "y" in "my".

au—like "ow" in "cow".

ei—like the "ay" in "hay" (Spanish only).

eu—a blend of "e" of "bet" and "u" of flute (Spanish only).

ia—like the "ya" of "yard" (Spanish only).

ie—like the "ye" of "yellow" (Spanish only).

io—like the "yo" of "yodel" (Spanish only).

iu—like "you" (Spanish only).

ua—like the "wa" in "want".

ue—like the "whe" in "where".

ui—like "we".

Consonants

b—as in "baby" (Spanish only).

c—like "k" before "a," "o" and "u"; like "s" before "e" and "i".

d—as in "dog" at the beginning of a word; like the "th" in "that" elsewhere (Spanish).

f—as in "four" (Spanish only).

g—like the "g" in "go" before "a," "o" and "u"; like "h" before "e" and "i" (Spanish).

h—silent before vowels; a glottal stop like the middle sound of "kitten" after vowels.

j—like "h," but harsher (Spanish only).

l—as in "like".

m—as in "moon".

n—as in "no".

ñ—roughly like the "ni" in "onion".

p—as in "pet".

r—like the "dd" in the American pronunciation of "ladder" (Spanish only).

s—as in "see" (Spanish only).

t—as in "ten".

v—like "b" in "baby" (Spanish only).

x—like "sh" in "she" (Nahuatl) or like "h" (Spanish only).

y—as in "yes".

z—like "s" in "see".

Digraphs (two letters always written together)

ch—as in "check".

cu/uc—"kw" as in "queen".

hu/uh—like "w" in "we".

ll—like "y" in "yes" (Spanish only).

qu—like "k" in "key".

rr—a "rolled r" (Spanish only).

tl—roughly like the "ttle" in "bottle".

tz—like the "ts" in "cats".

Note also that all Nahuatl (and most Spanish) words are stressed on the next-to-the-last syllable:

Anamacani—a/na/ma/CA/ni.

Maxaltic—ma/XAL/tic.

Tezcatlipoca—tez/ca/tli/PO/ca.

Quetzalcoatl—que/tzal/CO/atl.

GLOSSARY

Abyss, the—Amictlan, the lowest point of the Acapulco Trench.

ahuah—(pl. Ahuahqueh) A Lord of Water; another name for one of the tlaloqueh.

Ahuecapan—The depths of the sea, i.e., the region where the Atlacah live.

ahuitzotl—(pl. ahuitzomeh) "Water dog", a sort of magical aquatic creature with a hand at the end of its tail.

Air Sage—Ehcamatini, an atlacatl who can assume human shape.

Amictlan—See "Abyss, the".

Anamacani—The Princess of Tapachco; Air Sage and Royal Historian.

Apan—The Pacific Ocean.

Apixqueh—Guardians of all permanent entrances to Tlalocan.

apiyaztli—Sacred tunnels connecting temples or realms.

Aquimichin—Cihuacoatl and Minister of State for Tapachco; sister of Queen Iztalli; mother of Mihuah.

Archmage—Chief sorcerer.

Assembly of Calpolehqueh—The parliament of Tapachco.

atenhuatl—"River-dweller," an Air Sage who exiles himself to the human world.

atlacatl—(pl. Atlacah) A siren (mermaid) or triton (merman).

Atlan—Ancient island continent that sank 80,000 years ago.

Atlixco—"The Surface" or realm of human beings.

Atoyatl—Mythical current in the Deep that leads to the Abyss.

Botaben—Leader of a node of the Encante.

cehualli—See "shadow magic"

Cehuallocozcatl—See "Shadow Stone, the".

Celic—A former Royal Historian of Tapachco; monk of the Order of the Deep.

Cenaman—A marshal in the Royal Guard of Tapachco.

Chalchiuhtlicue—See "Matlalcueyeh".

Cihuacoatl—The title of the minister of state of Tapachco, see "Aquimichin".

chay abah—A large obsidian mirror used to travel between realms.

cocoah—Fraternal nagual twins, especially male-female pairs.

Compact of Blessed Creatures, the—A treaty among the major sentient races (humans, Little People, merfolk, the Encante, etc.) established by Quetzalcoatl at the beginning of the Fifth Age of the world.

Cuauhtemallan—Guatemala.

Dark Lord, the—See "Tezcatlipoca".

Deep, the—The ocean within the Acapulco Trench.

Ehcamatini—See "Air Sage".

Ellelli—A siren of Tapachco.

Encante, the—The collective name of a species of sentient pink river dolphins able to assume human form.

Enehnel—A member of the Royal Guard of Tapachco.

Epan Napotza—The emperor of Atlan; ancestor of every nagual and Ehcamatini; twin brother of Quelel Huetzo.

eztemalli—The blood magic of the tlacamichimeh.

Fatherless, the—The Ahtahtehqueh, a group of tlaloqueh expelled from Tlalocan.

Feathered One, the—See "Quetzalcoatl".

First Age, the—The era from the creation of the earth to its first destruction by Tezcatlipoca.

Fifth Age, the—The present era of history.

Fourth Age, the—The era during which Matlalcueyeh ruled the earth; destroyed by a flood.

Five Nations, the—The major merfolk kingdoms in the Pacific Ocean.

Green Magic—*Matlallotl*, the ability to manipulate living creatures, principally plants.

House of Napotza, the—A noble family in Tapachco that traces its roots back to the Emperor of Atlan.

Huitzilopochtli—The god of war.

Huixtocihuatl—Goddess of salt worshiped in Tapachco.

ihiyotl—The soul of emotions and passions; source of most magical power.

Ilancueh—A handmaiden of Princess Anamacani.

Iztac Teopixcacalli—The main monastery of the Order of the Deep.

Iztalli—The Queen of Tapachco.

Iyauhquemeh—A water elemental, one of Tlaloc's four generals.

Jabalí—The name given to the tlacamichin Rikar Tzaaq by a group of human children.

Jabalí Lagoon—A body of water in the Mexican state of Colima.

Jade Grimoire, the—A book of merfolk magic.

kamasotz—"Snatch-bat," a creature from the bowels of Mictlan.

Kihtyei—An ancient name for Guatemala.

Kisin—High Lord of Xibalba, capital city of Mictlan.

Little People, the—Tzapame, a race of elf-like beings.

Lord of Chaos, the—See "Tezcatlipoca".

man-fish—Literal translation of tlacamichin.

Matlalcueyeh—Goddess of water; also known as Chalchiuhtlicue; wife of Tlaloc.

matlallotl—See "Green Magic".

Maxaltic—The prince of Tapachco.

Mayahuel—Goddess of the maguey plant; the only tzitzimitl to renounce destruction and join with Quetzalcoatl.

Mictlan—See "Underworld, the."

Middle Apantic—An ancient language used by the tlacamichimeh.

Mihuah—A diplomat; daughter of Tapachco's Minister of State; the Queen's niece.

minamicqui—The deadliest jellyfish of the Deep.

Mintoc—A marshal in the Royal Guard of Tapachco.

Mrisu—A siren princess; wife of Epan Napotza.

nagual(es)—Shapeshifter(s); also nahualli.

nahualcuahuitl—A sorcerer's staff, used to channel and amplify magic.

nahualli—(pl. nahualtin) See "nagual".

Nalquiza—Tapachco's castellan (commander of the Royal Guard).

Nenotzalli in Tlayocoltzin, in—See "*Compact of Blessed Creatures, the*".

Nextic—King *of* Tapachco.

notapachicah—A specially bred sort of coral used in growing buildings in Tapachco.

Omelia—A former Royal Historian of Tapachco.

Order of the Deep, the—A group of monks and nuns from Tapachco who serve the goddess Huixtocihuatl.

Pacqui—Abbot of the monastery of the Order of the Deep.

Palace of Ministers—The building where the executive council of Tapachco lives and works

patolli—An ancient board game.

Pingo—One of the Little People; liaison with the Garza family.

Qucha Llaqta—An undersea kingdom off the coast of Peru.

Quelel Huetzo—Twin sister of Epan Napotza; found *the Shadow Stone* and caused Atlan to sink beneath the waves.

Quetzalcoatl—Lord of Creation and Order; brother of Tezcatlipoca.

Rikar Tzaaq—A tlacamichin, also known as Jabalí.

Robe of Mayahuel, the—A magical garment once belonging to the goddess Mayahuel that Carol can morph into multiple sets of clothing.

Roqha—An ancient name for the Atoyatl.

Royal Guard of Tapachco—A quasi-military force that guards the city of Tapachco.

Royal Historian—The atlacatl responsible for preserving, adding to, and retelling the history of the merfolk of Tapachco.

Savage Mages—The greatest of nagual twins, whose abilities were almost god-like.

sacred singer—Someone able to wield sacred song magic.

sacred song magic—Sorcery that uses singing to work spells.

shadow magic—The dark power of chaos wielded by Tezcatlipoca and his minions.

Shadow Stone, the—An ancient magical device capable of great destruction.

Sulamala—"Child of the Heart," one of the seven cities of Atlan.

Surface, the—See "Atlixco".

susto—The state of a person when the tonalli has left the body.

Tapachco—"Place of Coral," an undersea kingdom in the Pacific Ocean, built within large caverns in the mountain that forms the base of Isla Benedicto in the Revillagigedo Archipelago of the coast of Mexico.

Tapachcan—A native of Tapachco.

Tenamic—The Archmage of Tapachco; head of the court sorcerers.

teocuicani—See "sacred singer".

teocuicayotl—See "sacred song magic".

teotl—Divine energy found in all living things.

Tepeyollotl—"Mountain Heart," the nahualli of Tezcatlipoca; a massive jaguar.

Texoxqueh—See "Savage Mages".

teyolia—The spirit that lives on after a person's death.

Tezcatlipoca—Lord of destruction and chaos; brother of Quetzalcoatl.

tlacamichin—(pl. tlacamichimeh) A scaly, humanoid creature; man-fish.

Tlaloc—God of thunder, lightning, and water (especially rain).

Tlalocan—The realm of the god Tlaloc; a paradisiacal abode for certain human souls.

tlaloqueh—Water elementals created by the god Tlaloc; also known as ahuahqueh.

Tlatecuhtli—An earth god.

tonalli—A secondary spirit formed from teotl; the animal soul of a nagual.

tonal—A nagual's animal soul.

tzaccayotl—The magical illusion projected by merfolk to disguise themselves from humans.

tzapame—See "Little People, the".

tzapatzin—Singular form of tzapame.

tzitzimitl—(pl. tzitzimimeh) Star demon, a sort of destructive goddess capable of triggering an apocalypse.

Unazoko—An undersea kingdom off the coast of Japan.

Underworld, the—Mictlan, a nine-layered afterlife nestled among the roots of the World Tree presently controlled by Tezcatlipoca, though overseen by Lord and Lady Death.

wayxoc—(pl. wayxocob) Sentient sharks, serfs of the tlacamichimeh.

Water Dweller—See "Atlacatl."

World Tree, the—The axis of the universe, joining Mictlan, the earth and the thirteen heavens.

Xicol—A captain in the Royal Guard of Tapachco.

Xochiquetzal—The first wife of Tlaloc, mother of the tlaloqueh.

Xolotl—The nahualli of Quetzalcoatl; exists separately from the god now, mostly in the form of a large dog, in Mictlan.

Xomalloh—One of the Fatherless.

xoxal—Savage magic, a little-understood force possessed by twin shapeshifters.

Yayauhco—"Place of Eternal Dusk," the realm of Tezcatlipoca.

GUIDE TO SPANISH WORDS

Chapter 1

mojo—Wetback (offensive term for undocumented resident, shortened and Anglicized form of "mojado" or "wet").

cuate—Buddy (literally "fraternal twin").

¿Cómo te va en las clases?—How are you doing in your classes?

bien—Well.

Órale, pues—Okay, then.

curandera—Healer, shaman.

Pinche gringo—Damn white guy.

Güey, ahorita vas a ver que—Dude, right now you're going to see that.

Chale—No way.

pues or *pos*—Uh, well, you know (filler).

¿verdad, amores?—Right, my loves?

Claro que no, mamá—Of course not, Mom.

Ay, amor—Ah, my love.

Chapter 2

Sí, yo también te quiero, amor—Yes, I love you, too, dear.

Pero, ya—But anyway.

viejito—Little old man.

Lo típico—Typical stuff.

Chapter 3

M'ijo, ¿no te dije que dejaras esa cosa en casa?—Son, didn't I tell you to leave that thing at home?

Chapter 4

nagual—Shapeshifter.

Chapter 6

chiveado—Spoiled or stuck-up, but in a slightly embarrassed way.

Chapter 8

N'hombre—Literally "Nah, man," but more accurately meaning "to heck with that!"

cuates—Buddies, pals, friends.

Chapter 9

chaparrita—Shorty.

Chapter 10

amor—Love.

porrazo—Blow to the head with a club.

Chapter 11

Olvídalo—Forget it.

pulga—Flea market or open-air market.

Chapter 12

A la víbora, víbora—To the serpent, serpent.

de la mar, de la mar—Of the sea, of the sea.

por aquí pueden pasar—You can make your way through here.

Los de adelante corren mucho—Those in front run very fast.

y los de atrás se quedarán—Those in back will stay behind.

tras, tras, tras, tras—Hind, hind, hind, hind.

Una mexicana que fruta vendía—A Mexican woman selling fruit.

ciruela, chabacano, melón o sandía—Prunes, apricots, honeydew or watermelon.

Verbena, verbena, jardín de matatena—Vervain, vervain, a garden of jacks.

Verbena, verbena, la Virgen de la Cueva—Vervain, vervain, the Virgin of the Cave.

Campanita de oro déjame pasar—Little golden bell, let me through.

con todos mis hijos menos el de atrás—With all of my kids, except the one in back.

tras, tras, tras tras—Back, back, back, back.

Será melón, será sandía—It may be honeydew, may be watermelon.

será la vieja del otro día—May be the old fruit from the other day.

día, día, día, día—Day, day, day, day.

El puente está quebrado—The bridge is broken.

que lo manden componer—Tell someone to fix it.

con cáscaras de huevo—With lots of eggshells.

y pedazos de oropel—And bits of tin,

pel, pel, pel, pel—Tin, tin, tin, tin.

¡No manches, güey!—No freaking way, dude!

Chapter 14

O sea, estamos fritos—In other words, we're out of luck.

Chapter 16

Por poco se nos pasa—We almost missed it.

Chapter 20

m'ija—My daughter.

Chapter 21

Ay, dios mío—Oh, my God.

¡no lo hagas!—Don't do it!

Coda

Aprovechados—Scam artists.

el menso de tu hermano—Your brother the dork.

Ya basta, mamá—That's enough, Mom.

Ya párale, loca—Cut it out already, crazy person.

A product of an ethnically diverse family with Latino roots, David Bowles has spent most of his life in the Río Grande Valley, where he presently lives and works. Recipient of awards from the American Library Association, the Texas Institute of Letters and the Texas Associated Press, he has written several books, among them *Border Lore* and the Pura Belpré Honor Book *The Smoking Mirror*.